Kit and Ivy

A Red Team Wedding Novella by

Elaine Levine

Published by Elaine Levine
Cover art by Hot Damn Designs
Edited by Editing720
Copyright © 2014 Elaine Levine
All rights reserved.
Last Updated: 04-12-2014

Ebook Edition ISBNs:
ISBN-10: 0985420588
ISBN-13: 978-0-9854205-8-1

Print Book Edition ISBNs:
ISBN-10:0985420596
ISBN-13:978-0-9854205-9-8

DEDICATION

For Barry, always.

ACKNOWLEDGMENTS

Many thanks to Jenna and Susan, whose innovative use of the English language is inspiring. "Hungsome" and "metric fuck ton" have been added to the Red Team lexicon!

And a big thanks to Barbara and Michelle. I appreciate your willingness to drop everything and do a quick read whenever I need it!

A NOTE FROM THE AUTHOR:

We begin *Kit and Ivy: A Red Team Wedding Novella* at the point where *Honor Unraveled* finished. For enhanced enjoyment of this short story, be sure to read *The Edge of Courage*, *Shattered Valor*, and *Honor Unraveled* before starting this book!

—Elaine

OTHER BOOKS BY ELAINE LEVINE:

~Red Team Series~
(This series must be read in order)
1 The Edge of Courage (2012)
2 Shattered Valor (2012)
3 Honor Unraveled (2013)
3.5 Kit & Ivy, a Red Team Wedding novella
4 Twisted Mercy (coming 2014)
4.5 Ty & Eden, a Red Team Wedding novella
(coming 2014)
5 Assassin's Promise (coming 2014/2015)
5.5 Rocco & Mandy, a Red Team Wedding novella
(coming 2015)

~ Men of Defiance Series ~
(This series may be read in any order)
1 Rachel and the Hired Gun (2009)
2 Audrey and the Maverick (2010)
3 Leah and the Bounty Hunter (2011)
4 Logan's Outlaw (2012)
5 Agnes and the Renegade (2014)
6 Dulcie and the Bandit (coming 2015/2016)

CHAPTER ONE

Adam Banks stepped onto the front stoop before the man coming up his driveway could knock. From his office, he'd watched him get out of his unmarked black sedan and come toward the house. The man wore a nondescript charcoal suit—official government-issue.

Adam had been expecting a visit like this every day for thirteen years, but it was surreal to have it actually happen.

He wondered what news the man brought. Had his daughter committed a crime? Was she dead, a Jane Doe in a remote morgue, unclaimed, unwanted? What of his granddaughter? A niggling voice chastised him for even pretending to care. If he'd been a real father and grandfather, his daughter and granddaughter wouldn't be out in the world, alone.

"I'm looking for Adam Banks," the man in the suit

announced as he came up the front steps.

"And who might you be?" Adam asked.

"A messenger."

Adam stared at the man. "Got an ID?"

"No."

Adam's eyes narrowed. "Then state your business."

"Are you Adam Banks?"

"I am."

The man pulled an ivory envelope from an inside pocket and handed it to him. Adam closed the door behind him. He didn't want to trouble his wife with whatever news the man brought to their doorstep. He opened the unsealed envelope and withdrew the card inside.

"Ms. Ivy Banks and Mr. Kit Bolanger request the honor of your presence at their wedding..." The words jumped and blurred in front of him. He had to read the invitation twice.

"I'm required to wait for your answer," the suit told him.

"Kit didn't have the balls to come himself?"

"Is that your answer?"

"I'll be there."

"The invitation is for both you and your wife."

"We'll both be there."

"Very good, sir." The suit handed him another envelope. "Here is your itinerary and the number where you can reach Kit. A car like mine will pick you up two hours prior to your flight. You will be flown out and back on a private jet. A car will take you from the Cheyenne airport to the address in Wyoming where you'll be staying. You will arrive Thursday before the wedding and will depart Sunday. Do you have any questions?"

None the suit could answer. "No."

The suit nodded. "Good day, then, sir."

Adam closed the front door and walked back into the kitchen, where his wife was preparing their supper. "Who was that?" she asked as she stirred a pot on the stove.

Adam shook his head and picked up the day's stack of mail. "Some sales guy."

"This is a non-soliciting neighborhood. You'd think they wouldn't go door to door here."

He didn't respond. "How long before dinner?"

"Maybe a half-hour."

"I have to make a call. I'll be right back." He went down the hall to his office and shut the door. He took the invitation and itinerary out of his pocket and spread them across the desk. Anger expanded and twisted in his veins. He dialed Kit's number. It rang once.

"Bolanger, here."

Adam didn't answer. Part of him had been hoping his past hadn't just slammed into his present.

"Hello?"

"So it's true."

"Mr. Banks. You received the invitation, then."

"What the hell kind of game are you pulling now,

kid?"

"It's a wedding, Mr. Banks, not a game. I'm marrying your daughter. Will you be attending?"

"Your messenger didn't give you my answer?"

"He did. Thought perhaps you'd called to back out."

"This is cruel. Mrs. Banks has a weak heart. I can't bring her someplace where she'll be mistreated or stressed."

"I have no control over how she'll react to the weekend. I do know, for our part, you'll both be treated as honored guests. It's time to put the past behind us and move forward as a family."

"Ivy's agreeable to our visit?" There was momentary silence on the other end. "You haven't told her," Adam scoffed.

"No point worrying her if you weren't coming. I'll clear the way with her. However, I'm gonna say this only once: this is her special week, her special day. If you make her cry, if you insult or threaten her or hurt her feelings, I'll have your asses on a plane so fast, you won't know what hit you."

"What about the baby?"

"Casey's twelve now. She's as strong as her mother and very, very precious to both of us. My protection extends to her as well, feel me? You got an issue with me, you take it out with me. No matter what, you treat my girls like gold."

"Agreed. And likewise with Mrs. Banks."

"Agreed. See you in a couple of weeks." The line went dead.

Adam opened his office door, then started toward the kitchen, hoping by the time he got to the other side of the house he'd know what to tell his wife.

4

* * *

The locker room was steamy. And crowded. The entire Red Team, sans Max, were drying off and gearing up. Owen looked across the room and asked Kit, "You set a date yet for the big day?"

Kit grinned. "Yeah. Two weeks from this Saturday."

"Where are you getting married?" Kelan asked, toweling his hair.

"Here. Don't need the distraction of an offsite shindig. Besides, I want you guys there."

Kelan moved the towel aside and shook his head. "Don't do it here. Seriously, that's a bad choice."

"Why?" Kit frowned.

"Because we killed about a dozen bastards last month. And with all the weird shit Blade went through growing up, there's bad mojo here."

"Chill, K," Angel groaned. "There aren't any ghosts here."

"No, he's right." Blade looked at Kit. "There's something off with this house. Thought I was the only one who felt it."

Kit made a face. "I'm not delaying the wedding. You kidding? I only just got Ivy to agree to marry me. And we're not holding it somewhere else. The logistics are bad enough having it here."

"Let me bring a shaman in to clear and heal the space." Kelan looked between Kit and Owen.

"No," Owen nixed that idea. "No civilians. Or do the clearing, but keep it upstairs."

Kelan shook his head. "Won't work. Every inch of useable space has to be cleared, including the bunker, the basement, both main floors, all entrances and windows, stairs and elevator, and the grounds. What's here has to get pushed out and walled out."

Owen glared disbelievingly at him for an uncomfortably long moment. "No."

"Let him do it," Blade argued. "He's right. I got rid of the cage, but there are still shadows here. Have been for a while. I want them gone. And I want Kit's marriage to start on safe ground. He deserves it. Besides, it's not like this bunker is a secret. Our enemies spent a dozen years exploiting it before we took control of it."

Owen exchanged a glare with Kit, then capitulated. "Fine." He pointed at Kelan. "Your voodoo priests are never to be left alone anywhere in the building or on the grounds. And after their cleansing, we do a full security sweep." He shook his head. "And if shit goes down when they're here, they get the hell out of the way and let us do our business."

"It's not voodoo. He's a shaman. But I'll see that they're escorted," Kelan accepted Owen's terms.

"Can you make it happen before the wedding, K?" Kit asked.

Kelan nodded. "I'll make some calls and get it started."

"Let me know what it costs. I'll cover it," Kit told

him.

"No. It's my present to you."

Kit held his hand out to Kelan. "Ivy and I thank you."

Lockers slammed and the room grew quieter as the guys began leaving.

"You hear from Ivy's parents?" Blade asked as he and Kit walked to the main house.

"Yeah. They're coming."

"Huh." His gaze shot to Kit's face. "You break the news to Ivy?"

Kit sucked in a deep breath. "No. I wanted to be sure before I said anything. I was worried they'd still back out."

"You're a fucking idiot." Blade looked at Kit. "You do want Ivy to be at the wedding, right? 'Cause that ain't news she should be surprised with, like, the weekend of."

"I'll tell her. I just have to figure out how."

CHAPTER TWO

A light was still on in the kitchen. Kit looked at his watch. One a.m. Ivy had said two hours ago that she was coming to bed shortly. Obviously, she never made it. He stepped quietly into the kitchen, leaning against the doorjamb as he watched her work.

Bowls, mixers, blenders, piping tubes, and other tools were scattered across the counter, along with various sweet and savory ingredients. The kitchen smelled divine, like a French patisserie and delicatessen combined.

Ivy was frowning down at something she was preparing. Her dark hair was pinned up, but after the long hours spent in the kitchen, several tendrils had escaped and now lingered by her face in ways that irritated her and heated him. Kit smiled, feasting on the sight of her. He shifted his weight, crossing his bare feet as he leaned against the entranceway.

She looked up, then registered what his presence meant. "Oh." She glanced at the clock, seeing that several hours had passed since she said good night. "Oh!" She sent a panicked look across the counter. "Kit, I'm sorry—"

He crossed the room to stand behind her and massage her tight shoulders. "Don't apologize."

"I wanted to test out some treats for the wedding. I don't want to be in Kathy's way in here during the day, so I have to do it after her shift ends." She moaned as he worked her stiff muscles. "That's heaven."

"Why don't you use Mandy's kitchen?"

Ivy gave him a dark look. "I can't cook there. She doesn't have half the tools I need and it's too small."

He drew her back to lean against him and wrapped his arms around her. "What can I do to help?"

"Try this." She cut into a roast baked in a weave of bacon strips.

Kit took the bite from her fork. "Oh, man. That's it." He went for a second taste. "What is that?"

"Pork loin stuffed with apples, mushrooms, kale, and my secret sauce. Like it?" She fed him a bite from a little fried ball of something. "And potato fritters." He took up a fork and had another bite. "Like it?"

"Yeah."

"That's option A. This is option B." She cut into a small, layered tower of something topped with petite lettuce leaves.

"Why do we need an option B?"

"Because not everyone likes pork. Or eats meat. I thought I'd serve a fish and a vegetarian something."

Kit laughed. "Honey, you've seen the guys eat. They don't even chew their food, just wolf it down. They'll eat whatever. Don't kill yourself over this." She gave him a wounded look, which made him wish he'd said just about anything else.

"I want this to be special. I want our friends to remember how elegant the day was. I want it to be an *event*."

"Okay." He took the taste she was offering him. "That's good. What is it?"

"Crab and Lobster Louie."

"I like it. It's pretty, all those colors."

Ivy bit her bottom lip. "You're patronizing me."

"Never. This is a very nice dish. Besides, if the guys have to use eating utensils, it'll absolutely slow them down long enough to enjoy your tireless culinary labors." He grinned at her.

"All right." She sighed and looked around the room. "I just need to work out a vegan dish. Then I can start on the desserts and hors d'oeuvres."

"But not tonight. You have time. I'll ask Kathy if she could perhaps share the kitchen with you for the next couple of days while you hammer out the menu. How about we clean up in here? Then I'm taking you to bed." He started gathering dishes. "You are ordering the wedding cake, aren't you, not making it yourself?" He frowned at her.

"I am. I still have to decide on the cake and

flowers." She gave him a desperate look. "And a dress. I need a dress. And Casey has nothing appropriate to wear." She swiped the hair from her face. "This is happening so fast."

He leaned over and kissed her temple, getting a taste of flour. "Anything you have in your closet will be perfect."

"Kit, I'm never going to have another wedding. I want it to be special."

"Then go shopping, find the perfect dress. Whatever you're happy with, I'll be happy with. I've added you to my bank accounts. Your credit card is in my room. Do some damage."

"Seriously?"

He nodded. "But take Selena with you. You still have to be careful and aware."

He went to the dishwasher and started loading. *Now tell her*, he prompted himself. *Now would be a good time.* Kit looked at her. She was wrapping up the dishes she'd made and putting them in the far back of the sub-zero to hide them from the guys. She didn't want them to preview the food and ruin their surprise on the big day.

Fuck. This was not the ideal time. She was wound tight enough to break. If he told her now, when she was exhausted...well, it was just a bad plan. Tomorrow would be better. He'd tell her tomorrow.

* * *

"How are the wedding plans going, Ivy?" Val asked after dinner the next day. Casey had taken Zavi to watch TV; it was just the adults at the table, lingering with coffee. Kit gritted his teeth, hoping the guys kept their mouths shut about her parents.

"Pretty well. I think I have most of the menu ironed out. I worked on choosing the decorations and the cake today. Now we just need dresses. I think we'll make a trip out for them sometime this week."

"Val can help with that," Eden said as she sipped her coffee.

Val held up his hands, sending Blade a grin. "No can do. You girls are off limits, apparently, in this establishment."

Eden punched Blade's arm. "What did you say to him?"

Blade glared at Val. "Nothing. I just explained his boundaries."

Kit smiled, remembering the black eye Blade had given Val after he'd taken Eden shopping. "Iv, do you want Val's help picking a dress?" Things had been quiet with the White Kingdom Brotherhood. They could spare the sniper for a day.

She looked at Kit, then Val. "Well—"

Eden sighed. "This isn't an ordinary event, Ivy. It's a wedding. You *need* Val. None of us know how to pick out a wedding dress. And shoes. We don't even know where to shop for what you're looking for."

"What kind of dress do you want, Ivy?" Val asked.

"Something simple and elegant—a dress Audrey

12

Hepburn would have worn last century."

"Vintage, then." He thought for a minute. "I do know the perfect shop in Denver." He looked at Kit. "I bet I could get the owner to close it down for us for a day."

"You'll love what he can find for you," Fee told Ivy.

"He's like a fairy godmother," Eden added. "You've seen what he did for me."

Val leaned back in his seat. He spread his arms out, hooking his hands on the backs of Eden and Fee's seats, and grinned a challenge at Kit.

"How the hell do you know about a vintage dress shop in Denver?" Selena asked, but then a thought occurred to her. She sat up and focused in on him. "Wait—you're a secret cross-dresser, aren't you?"

He grinned. "At least *I'm* not afraid of my feminine side. I am what I am, Sel. You should come, too. I'll find the perfect ensemble for you."

"You're letting him go?" Kelan asked Kit.

Kit made a face as he looked around the table at the expectant faces of the women. He shrugged. "It's his friend's shop. And it looks as if the ladies want him to go." He gave Val a hard look. "You better respect the boundaries."

Val grinned. "Got it. No dressing rooms."

Kelan put his napkin on the table. "If he's going, I'm going."

Owen shook his head. "No."

"Selena'll have the front. Val'll have his head you

know where. I'll guard the back."

"They're shopping for dresses, K. It's not a fucking mission," Owen growled.

"Call it what you want." Kelan shrugged. "Selena's good—damn good—but she can't hold things down alone if shit breaks loose. Someone has to have her back."

Kit sighed. "Agreed. You go with them, K."

* * *

Fiona stepped out of her room. Eden's door was open—she could hear the girls talking inside as she went by. Tank was suited up in his official-looking red work vest.

"You won't believe the day Val has organized for us, Fee," Ivy told her after calling her into the room. Val had gotten the owner to rearrange her schedule so they'd have the whole shop for as long as they needed. And he'd had her bring in mani/pedi stations and a couple seamstresses so that any needed modifications could be made on the spot. He'd also had her cater refreshments and lunch. "It's going to be like a day at the shopping spa for us!"

Fee was shocked at how thoughtful and thorough Val had been. She'd been hoping to get a shopping trip with him ever since he took Eden—today would be awesome. She had the money Rocco and Mandy had been paying her to take care of Zavi this summer. She'd been saving it for school, but she should be able to take some to cover a new dress and a pair of shoes. She hoped. Val had expensive tastes. If the clothes weren't within her means, she'd have to pick something in her current wardrobe.

"Are you ready?" Eden asked the room at large.

"I couldn't decide what to wear," Fee told the others. "Do I look okay?"

"Ohhh." Eden grinned. "A whole day with Kelan, huh?"

Fee made a face. "Do I?" She caught her reflection in Eden's mirror. She was wearing an airy sundress in a light cotton fabric. She checked her bejeweled leather flip-flops, making sure they worked with the dress. Her blond hair was growing out from the bob she'd had when she first came to the team.

Eden hooked her arm through Fee's and led her into the hallway. "You look like a princess. You always do."

Kelan was in the foyer, waiting with Selena and the others. His eyes met hers as she came down the stairs. She smiled but he did not. A wash of heat colored her face—so frustrating when she most wanted to appear cool and unaffected.

Kit was assigning people to the two SUVs they were taking for the day: Val and all the girls in one, Kelan, Selena, Eden, and Tank in the other. When Fee heard that, her gaze flew to Kelan. She wanted him to argue, rearrange things, make it so that she could go with him.

He didn't and, as the group exited, she held back.

Kit moved down the hallway, returning to the den. She yearned for a few seconds of being near Kelan; stolen moments, like this, were all she would get today. Why she tortured herself, she didn't know; he obviously didn't feel any urgency to spend time with her.

She looked at him over her shoulder, anger and frustration seething within her. He followed her to the door, but before they could step outside, he wrapped a hand about her waist. He drew her back against him and shut the door, keeping one hand on it as he leaned over her.

"Don't be upset, Fiona. I'm on duty. If you were to ride with me, I'd be thinking about nothing but you." He nuzzled her hair as he spoke, his low voice rumbling into her ear, whispering against something deep within her. "I will anyway. But if you're with me, the temptation to touch you would be a severe distraction. You unman me, Fiona."

Her blood became electrified, tingling everywhere he touched. Her mind echoed the vibrations of his growled words. He opened the door. Cool morning air spilled inside, pulling her back to reality.

"One more thing, Fiona." She turned and looked up at him. "I'm not happy that Val's going to be helping you shop, but I sure as hell am not letting him pay for your selections. Choose what you like. It's on me."

"Kelan—I can't. I have some money set aside. I can pay for myself—Val never was going to pay for me."

He bent a finger beneath her chin and lifted her face so that her eyes had no choice but to meet his. "Save your money for school. Think of today as a gift for me. Seeing you happy gives me joy. Please."

She took a step away from him, unable to have a coherent thought standing so close to him. She shook her head. "I have no defenses against you."

"Nor should you, my other half."

As his words slipped through her mind and down into her heart, she smiled at him. She went back and reached up to kiss his cheek and whisper, "I think you should know I'm falling very, very hard for you."

CHAPTER THREE

Selena walked into the dress shop with Kelan, Eden, and Tank. Val and the other women were in the SUV out front, waiting for the shop to be cleared.

The sign on the door read, "Closed for Private Showing." Window shades, in Martha Stewart mint green, had been lowered across the front. The room they walked into was a study in green pastels and ivory. The antique Persian carpet was in subdued but rich tones of gold and aqua. The French, off-white upholstered chairs and settees were trimmed in gilded wood, a nice complement to the feminine decor. Arranged along the walls were glass showcases of headless modernistic mannequins, in varying skin tones, wearing stunning wedding attire, a mix of historical, vintage, and contemporary. Selena felt as if they'd stepped into the wedding wing of a textiles museum.

A banquet table stood against one set of display cases with an assortment of china trays and cake stands filled with delicate sandwiches, *petit fours*, cupcakes, fruits, and salad choices. Tall urns of coffee and hot water were placed on another table with a selection of teas. Yet another table offered fluted glasses of champagne. Selena glared at Kelan. Apparently, Val didn't understand what keeping the day low-key meant.

A woman came forward to greet them. Her shoulder-length blond hair barely moved as she walked. Trim and coiffed, she looked like a barracuda—or some senator's wife. She was classy enough not to give Selena's beige tee and cargo pants a dismissive once-over. Nor did she get hung up on the weapons she and Kelan wore.

The woman held out her hand of long, manicured nails. "I'm Lisa. You must be with Val." The bracelets on the woman's wrist jangled as she shook hands with Selena and the others.

"I'm Selena. That's Kelan. And that's Eden. Mind if we have a look around before things get started?"

She didn't seem surprised by that request. "Of course. I'll give you the tour, then we can begin when you're ready."

They went through room after room, each with themed dresses for women and children and ensembles for men. It was a rabbit warren of lace, silk, and satin attire, in equal numbers of new and gently used garments—including the vintage apparel

Ivy wanted.

The dressing rooms were large spaces with elegant armchairs and mirrors on each wall. They opened onto a wide room with three round platforms, again surrounded by mirrors.

"We've placed our seamstresses in here for the day. Any alterations that are needed can be done immediately." The next segment of the shop held an extensive array of high-heel shoes, purses, wraps, jewelry, lingerie, and wedding party decorations and supporting items. "We've placed our manicurists in the shoes and accessories area." She looked at Selena's short-nailed hands. "I hope you'll take advantage of them as well."

Selena gave her a disinterested look. "Is that the extent of the premises?"

Lisa nodded. "That's it for the front rooms. There are offices and restrooms in the back hall, this way." As they headed in that direction, she explained about their exits. "We have four external doors, all of which are locked from the outside, and today, they function as emergency exits. We won't be disturbed."

Selena returned to the front to take Eden and Tank through the rest of the space so they could check for weapons and explosives. When the dog found no hidden dangers, Kelan took up a post near the primary back exit. Selena radioed Val the all clear, then went to hold the door for the women.

Val followed the women into the store. He ignored Selena but gave Lisa a big smile and greeted her warmly with a kiss on each cheek. He put his arm around her and turned to face the women. "Well? What do you think?"

"Val—this is amazing," Ivy answered. "What a wonderful discovery this shop is. Look how elegant everything is. I'm impressed."

"Lisa's shop is magical. She always has that perfect ensemble for whatever function you need to attend." He smiled at Lisa, giving her shoulders a slight squeeze.

"Thank you," Ivy said to the both of them.

"I'll show you around, ladies," Lisa said. "Then, please, help yourselves to refreshments at any time. This won't be a short visit, so I want you to keep your strength up!"

Selena held her position at the front of the store as Val followed the women into the next room. The salesgirls who stayed up front followed him with their eyes, then exchanged glances with each other and giggled. She ground her teeth together. Why the man had such an effect on every female he encountered, Selena refused to contemplate; he couldn't have done them all. She glanced down at Eden's dog. His big yellow eyes looked up at her. Whatever. She was in good company guarding the front entrance.

She could hear the delighted comments from Ivy and her friends as they moved from room to room. Lisa was giving them the spiel about colors and themes and choices for the bridal party. After a while, things got quiet, presumably because the girls were heading to the dressing rooms.

Val came back to the front room. He smiled at her as he held up his hands. "I'm staying out of the dressing rooms. You can report back to Kit." He poured a cup of coffee. "Want some?"

"No thanks."

He walked up to her and smiled. "Go back and join them. I've got your post."

"Forget it. I've a job to do."

"You do. Picking out an outfit for Ivy's wedding."

"I'm not going to her wedding."

"Of course you are. The entire household is. You're going. And you're not going in tactical gear."

"Someone has to be on guard duty."

He ignored that. "I've selected a couple of things for you to try. If they don't work for you, let me know. I'll find something else. There will be no forgotten Cinderellas at Ivy's ball."

"I fucking hate fairytales."

"Why?"

"Because they showcase the ideal of women being dependent on men."

"You got a problem with men helping women? Women help men all the time. It doesn't lessen the men in any way."

"I have a problem pinning all my hopes on men."

He lifted a brow. "You pin all your hopes on women?"

"I pin all my hopes on me."

"Then you're in good company. Go. Try the

outfits on. Don't worry about prices. Owen's treating. He knows you can't afford them on a soldier's salary."

She stood her ground. Ivy came out, followed by Mandy and Casey. She was wearing a vintage gown of white silk with a fitted bodice, a wide peach satin sash, and a flaring skirt with layers of crinolines. She wore nude, slightly tinted hose and white satin pumps. A multi-strand pearl necklace dressed up the simple bodice. She walked up to Val and turned around.

"What do you think?"

He tilted his head, considering her outfit. "I think you look beautiful. But that's not the dress."

"Okay. I'll be right back."

For the next two hours, the girls presented themselves to Val in ensemble after ensemble. When they got frustrated, he helped them refine their choices until each had an outfit she adored.

"Why do you make them keep trying things on when everything they've come out in is gorgeous?" Selena asked when there was a lull in the modeling.

Val was seated in a green sateen chair that swiveled. He turned and looked at her. "I'm not sending them back. They know when they come out that it's not quite the right dress. I'm not deciding anything for them. I can see in their eyes if they love what they're wearing. And when they do, I will, too. I only mirror their thoughts."

Ivy came out in a stunning floor-length dress. The

design was classic and feminine. The outer shell was a sleeveless ivory lace from the V-neck to the hem, with a solid ivory sheath beneath that fell only to mid-calf. Light sifted through the lace by her ankles. A simple white sash banded her narrow waist.

Val pulled in a long breath. "That's it. It's perfect."

"You like it?"

"Oh, yeah."

She smoothed her hands down her hips. "I love it. It's elegant. Understated."

"It's perfect. Kit won't be able to take his eyes off you."

The other girls came out in their final outfits, all in complementary shades of ivory and beige and cream. Casey's had a faint print of dusky roses and champagne satin straps. Eden's was a simple dress of lined eyelet lace with short sleeves and a scooped neck. It hit mid-thigh, making her short legs seem longer than they were. Mandy's was a flowing muslin dress with a wide sash that was laced at the waist. Her sleeves were cut away at the elbows. Fiona chose a sundress with a skirt made from three layers of different types of lace, ending above the knees. Very different dresses for very different women.

Val looked from one woman to the next. He shook his head. "You're breathtaking independently, but together you look like a bouquet of women. So beautiful. I'm lucky I got to spend this day with you. What about shoes?"

"We'll do that next. Selena hasn't selected her

outfit yet," Ivy told him.

Val turned in his chair and looked at Selena. They all were looking at her. Jesus, that was uncomfortable. "I'm not coming to the wedding."

Ivy frowned. "Why not? Do you have to be somewhere else?"

"No." Selena braced herself for the arguments that would be lobbed at her.

"Don't you want to come?"

She frowned at the women, seeing their expectant faces. "I'm not in Wolf Creek Bend for social reasons. I'm there to work."

Ivy shook her head and came forward. "That's nonsense. We're all there for work. And we're all coming to the wedding." She took hold of Selena's wrist and led her back into the dressing rooms area. They were surprisingly neat given how many different outfits the girls had tried on. The staff had worked hard to keep everything organized. Two outfits she hadn't yet seen on any of the women were hanging on one of the dressing room doors.

"Val picked these for you," Eden told her.

"He doesn't know my size."

Ivy opened the dressing room door for her. "I bet he figured it out; he did with us. Try them on. And he said Owen was paying for your outfit, so you don't have to worry about the cost. Just see if you love it. You're coming to the wedding, Selena."

"Do you want help changing?" Fee asked.

She made a face, glancing around at each of the

women. "No."

"Then we'll go get your shoes. What size do you wear?"

"Eight."

Fee hurried off. "We're on it!"

Selena removed her gun from its holster and set it on the table, then sat down and removed her boots and socks. What a pain in the ass this was. Far easier to just stay in her room and avoid the whole wedding thing. She was hoping she'd have been able to return to regular duty by now, but Owen had had her tour extended for some reason.

She stripped to her bra and panties, then looked at the two outfits Val had chosen. She was surprised he'd picked pantsuits for her. Maybe he'd guessed—correctly—there was no way in hell she'd wear a skirt.

The first outfit was made of a taupe linen. The pants were high waisted and wide-legged with a thin cuff at the hem. The top was a sleeveless vest with suit lapels and a striped pattern of darker and lighter taupe tones. She put it on and looked at herself from the front, then the side. She flexed her shoulders. It fit comfortably, let her move easily. It showed her curves, hugging her breasts and slim torso. She peeked at the price: $375. She laughed. Served Owen right to have to pay so much for an outfit she'd only wear once.

"Selena? I have some shoes for you," a saleslady called through the door. "Oh! I like that!" she said when Selena opened the door. The girls, still in their wedding clothes, gathered around.

"Come out here and let us see you," Ivy urged.

"Let me get some shoes on." Selena looked through the boxes of shoes and selected a pair of black high-heeled sandals with a wide band across the toes. She tucked her gun in the waistband, then opened the door and stepped outside into the mirrored room with the seamstresses.

At five foot eight barefoot, the heels made her almost a head taller than some of the other girls. Selena liked the advantage her height gave her. In crowded spaces, she could see across a deeper area of a room since she didn't have to look through walls of people but could look over their heads.

"Wow," Ivy said. "Just wow. You look fabulous. Do you like it?"

Selena thought about Val's words, how he knew when a woman loved what she was wearing. She wasn't sure she loved it, but she did like it. It was comfortable. And it looked good on her. "I can move in it. I haven't been out of ops clothes in so long, I'm not sure I know what I like. It's expensive."

"Don't worry about that. Owen's got it covered," Ivy told her. She gestured for her to turn around.

"How can you wear those heels?" Eden asked.

"I like them." Selena grinned. "They're terrific weapons in hand-to-hand. If something goes down at the house, all contact will be in a close-quarters fight."

Eden laughed. "I wish I had your grace."

"You have a different function." She looked at the

dog trainer. "Those cowboy boots are a beautiful contrast to the softness of your dress. It works."

"That's what Mandy said."

"What about the other outfit Val picked?" Fiona asked.

Selena shrugged. "It has ruffles. Fucking ruffles. No."

Ivy laughed. "Just try it on. I didn't expect to choose a floor-length dress, but it was one of the ones Val picked."

Selena went back into the dressing room and switched outfits. The second ensemble was another taupe pantsuit, this one of brushed satin in a champagne color. The pants were low-rise, hugging the middle of her hips. They had a wide cuff at the bottom that hung open like a slouchy hem. The top was a jacket of the same material with cutaway sleeves edged in sheer chiffon just a shade lighter than the satin. The lapel was made of the same chiffon, loose enough to make gentle folds as it framed the neckline. The chiffon lapels ended in a large bow where the jacket sides met. The tails of the bow draped down longer than the jacket hem. Three buttons closed the jacket, right at her breasts, leaving it open above and below. The lower edges of the jacket were cut at an angle so that it spread apart over her stomach, exposing her navel and hinting at bare skin between the jacket and the hip-high trousers.

She looked at herself, shocked that she would like such a feminine outfit. There was a large ornamental rose in the middle of the bow, which she hated, but the rest she loved. She dug through the shoeboxes again and found a pair of strappy stiletto sandals. The white satin didn't do anything for her, but maybe she could find something like them in a better color.

She opened the door and stepped out to the women. Their eyes widened as they looked her over from head to foot. Uncertain what their shocked silence meant, she filled it with her own assessment.

"I hate the flower."

Lisa nodded toward one of the seamstresses, who hurried over to remove the rose. "You could wear a large brooch there instead. Something in amethyst or pearl."

Selena looked at herself, imagining the jacket with something else in place of the flower. She looked at Ivy and Casey. "Say something."

Ivy brought her hands to her mouth and shook her head. "I can't. I'm speechless."

"Take your hair down," Mandy suggested, coming over to hold a hand out for the clips and bobby pins that held Selena's dark hair in a tight twist. Her heavy hair fell down, drifted about her shoulders and spilled down her back.

Fiona clapped her hands. "Selena, you're gorgeous. You have to take that outfit."

"You don't think it's too much?"

"Too much what?" Ivy asked. "Too stunning?"

"Go show Val. You have to show him," Eden urged.

"No."

"Please, Selena. You'll know it's a hit when you see his face."

"I don't need his approval."

"Oh, go on. What are you afraid of?" Ivy challenged her.

Selena made a face. "Fine."

"Wait! Let us get out there first," Eden said. "I want to see his face." The girls hurried out the dressing room exit.

Selena bent her neck this way and that, easing some of the strain from her shoulders. The girls had abandoned her. She looked back at Lisa, who gave her an encouraging nod. Refusing to hide in the dressing room, she put her shoulders back and walked down the corridor to the front room where Val sat.

His eyes locked on her midsection as she stepped in front of the women. His face tightened. He hadn't looked at her eyes once. *Freakin' liar, Mr.-I-mirror-their-thoughts fashionista.*

"Walk toward me," he ordered, motioning her forward with a wave of his hand.

Oh. She so did not like doing this, but her feet had a mind of their own. She moved toward him with a slow prowl. He seemed fascinated with the way the jacket shifted over her waist and hips, hiding and exposing her navel. His blue eyes went dark as he looked her over from head to toe. He came to his feet.

Selena lifted her chin, prepared to take the outfit

30

regardless of his reaction. Why the hell she was submitting to his perusal, she didn't know. Too late to turn back now. He stood not a foot from her and looked down into her eyes.

"This is the one." She didn't answer him, didn't want her agreement to be taken as submission when she'd already chosen this outfit. "What happened to the rose?"

"I ditched it."

"I've brought you a selection of brooches so that the heart of the bow won't seem bare," Lisa said, indicating a velvet-lined tray one of her assistants held.

Val looked over the choices on the tray. He picked the very one Selena liked. It had a huge, halved pearl circled by several other smaller pearls set off by a dozen even smaller amethysts. He looked at Selena as he handed the brooch to the salesgirl. Selena didn't look away from him as the salesgirl pinned the brooch where the rose had been, between her breasts. When the girl stepped back, Val's gaze moved down Selena's chest on its way to the pearl pin. His nostrils flared. Without looking away from her, he gave Ivy an order.

"She sits at my table."

Ivy shook her head. "Sorry, Val. Owen's already made it clear she's to sit with him."

He did look at Ivy then. "Owen can join us."

"Yeah. I don't think I'm going to get between you two," Ivy said. "I already have the seating plan figured out."

"Then change it. If you want me to deal with Owen, I will."

"Oh, for crissakes. I'm not a toy for you and Owen to fight over. Ivy, I'll choose my own table."

"There's no need to worry about it. I'll work it out," Ivy told her. "I love your outfit. The guys won't know what to make of you."

"They'll make nothing of her. She's our teammate," Val snapped. To Lisa, he said, "I like her shoes, but the color's wrong."

"That's not a problem. I can have these dyed and then overnight them to you."

Selena was just looking down at the price tags for the outfit and the pin when Val said they'd take her ensemble. This suit was twice the price the other one was, and the brooch was three times the price.

"No. This is too much. I'll take the other one."

"Owen can buy your outfit. I'll buy the brooch," Val said.

Selena shook her head. "You don't get to buy me things."

"You don't get to tell me how to spend my money." He stared at her, daring her to argue with him. "When did you last—or ever—have an outfit as perfect as this for an event?"

"I don't go to events."

"You'll be at one on Saturday." He grinned. "I want to see Owen's face when I get the first dance with you."

"I don't dance."

Val's smile died as the edge in his eyes tightened his face. "First time for everything."

She unpinned the brooch and set it back on the tray. She started to unbutton one of the three buttons fastening her jacket. Val's eyes were on the skin her hands exposed. "You want to go broke to torture the boss, find a different plaything. I'm wearing the freakin' rose." She turned from the group and went back to the dressing rooms.

CHAPTER FOUR

Selena dove into the pool in the gym building later that night. It was late. The house was quiet. Her time was finally her own. Spending the day with Val and the girls had left her edgy. She thought a few laps would help work out the knots. She'd gotten only two laps in when someone else dove into the pool. She looked into the lane next to her. It was one of the guys.

She wasn't swimming in a rush, more leisurely enjoying stretching out in the quiet solitude of the water. The other swimmer was going in the opposite direction. When he hit the other end of the pool and turned around, she saw him lift out of the water to pull air.

Owen.

Selena focused on her strokes. He passed her. She sped up, catching up with him before the end of the lane. They turned and kicked off the wall at virtually the same time. Then for six more laps they kept pace. Selena was beginning to feel winded. She imagined Owen was as well. She kicked forward, pushing hard, wanting to beat him to the end of the pool. As soon as she thought it, she worried about beating her boss. Outperforming your superiors was rarely a good thing. She was so damned competitive. There were few men who could outdo her in most endurance sports. She didn't like yielding, but this was her freakin' boss—albeit a temp boss.

She ended up slowing down for just a fraction of a second, long enough for him to finish before her. They both stood up. She looked up at him and smiled, then swallowed the gesture when he didn't return it. He looked angry, actually. Great. Was this his private pool time?

He gripped the edge of the pool and hoisted himself out. She watched a pair of long, lean legs pull out of the water, capped by a tight ass in a Speedo. She hated male bikinis, even though he had the body for it with his V-shaped chest, lean hips, and taut thighs. He walked straight over to the bench and grabbed his towel, giving her an eyeful of the rest of his body when he turned around. And wasn't that just what she'd needed to know: her boss was hungsome. The cold water had caused no shrinkage. How he kept it all in there, she didn't know. He was toweling his hair. God, she hoped he hadn't seen her sneak a peek. He moved the towel. His mood didn't look much improved. She kept her eyes at his face, going no lower than his mouth. Well, to the cleft in his chin—

"You held back."

He'd caught that? "Yeah." She grinned. "Didn't want to hurt your feelings."

"Fuck my feelings. I'd rather be beaten by someone better than me than forfeited to by that same person. Feels like cheating. Don't do it again."

"Roger that."

They exchanged a look. Eventually, he nodded at her, then started for the locker room door.

"Hey, Owen." He stopped and looked back at her. "Thanks for the outfit today."

"You find something you liked?"

She lifted herself from the water. He apparently had none of her reservations about doing a once-over. She picked up a towel, dried her face, then draped it over her neck; she'd be damned if she'd hide behind it. Even if his gaze fired up her nerves in strange ways. "Yeah, but it was expensive."

Owen shrugged. "Your money."

"What do you mean?"

"I'll be providing you with a bonus equal to the cost I'll be deducting from your next check."

"Huh. Maybe you coulda said something sooner. I might have decided to use that money differently." She walked up to him.

"That wasn't an option." He looked down into her eyes. "I'm glad you're coming to the wedding."

"Why'd you ask to have me sit at your table?"

A muscle ticked in his jaw. Perhaps she wasn't supposed to know that. "You're a guest on the team. It's my job to see that you adjust to your assignment here."

"I don't understand what my assignment is."

"You will." He walked into the men's locker room, and damn if she didn't watch until he disappeared behind the door. She sighed. It would be a good thing, a really good thing, if she finished up here before everything got weird.

* * *

Ivy pulled the latest secret wedding samples out of the fridge and handed them to Kathy. The two of them had kept the guys from grazing on Ivy's test recipes through the week by getting them out of the house as soon as possible each day.

"I know you've been testing more dishes than you'll actually serve, Ivy, but you've got enough food for an army here!" Kathy commented as she filled a shopping bag with plastic containers full of Ivy's delicious test recipes.

"I know. I just want everything to be perfect."

"It will be. Carla and I will handle the serving and Dennis will man the bar."

"No." Ivy looked over as she shut the fridge door. "You and Dennis are going to join us, aren't you?"

"We'll be there. But I don't want you worrying

about anything or running around and not enjoying yourself. Leave the running to me and Carla. That way we don't need to have strangers here. It's best, really, given the situation."

"But I wanted you to enjoy yourself, too. After all you do for us—"

"There's nothing I love more than a party. Let me do this for you and Kit." She reached over and took Ivy's hand. "Ivy, the people who care about you get to pitch in and help. That's what family does. And right now, we're family."

Ivy had to fight back tears. "Thank you."

"What have you decided about decorations and flowers?"

"We ordered the flowers from the florist in town. They're being delivered Friday."

"And music?"

"Greer's playing DJ."

"Have you decided if you're going to set up tables outside or eat in the dining room?"

"I think we'll be setting up tables outside on the lawn, then we'll use the terrace for dancing."

Kathy nodded. "I'll be sure to get the tablecloths ready. How many tables will you need?"

"I think we'll have about forty here."

"Oh! So many. I'm glad I asked. I'll need to rent place servings, then."

"I know. I wanted to keep it small, but I can't ignore my crew from the diner. And there are a couple of folks in town who are coming—the sheriff and the doctor and their dates."

"That's wonderful. I only knew about your parents. I guess we'll need seven tables, then."

Ivy went still. "What do you mean my parents?"

"Well, of course they'll be here. They're your parents."

"I didn't invite them."

"Oh. Oh." Kathy went pale and gave her a panicked look. "I must have gotten something mixed up. Don't worry about it--mistake. We have enough of everything if we have to make last-minute adjustments. I know where we can rent covers for folding chairs—same place as the dishes. We've had to do that a time or two for Ty's father." She paused, then corrected herself. "Or the man we thought was his father."

Ivy was rattled by the mention of her parents, but Kathy seemed to be truly thinking out loud, not speaking from actual knowledge. Or was she? "I think we're all set. Can you and Carla handle that many people?"

"Absolutely. Dennis will help, too. But if you like, I could see if Carla's two daughters are available to help?"

"Yes. I think so. Be sure to give their information to Greer, though. Just to follow protocol."

"Of course."

"Good night, Kathy. Thank you for taking care of the food. I'm glad you have people to give it to."

"Oh, yes. The folks at the retirement home in

town have been enjoying your hard work all week. They'll be sad to see the end of your samples. Good night, dear. I can't wait for Saturday."

"Night, Kathy."

* * *

Kit was in the hallway when Ivy stepped out of the kitchen. He pulled her into a hug then kissed her forehead. "We need to talk."

She drew back and looked up at him. The tension in his face set off alarms. "What's wrong?"

"Nothing's really *wrong*. There are just some things we need to discuss."

"About the wedding?"

"Yeah."

"You're not postponing, are you?"

"Never." He took her hand and led her through the kitchen to the large patio in the back. He took out his phone and tapped an app.

"What are you doing?"

"Just giving us some privacy. Greer set up an app to manage our security systems. I'm shutting down the eyes and ears out here."

Ivy folded her arms and tried to keep herself calm. "Kit, you're scaring me."

He faced her and took hold of her hands. "You're not going to like what I have to say to you."

"I'm not really liking the anticipation either. Just say it."

"I reached out to your parents."

"No." His steady gaze told her he wasn't making it up. "Why would you do something like that?"

"I invited them to the wedding."

The air left Ivy's lungs in a huff of disbelief. "You did what?" He didn't repeat himself. He didn't need to. His words lingered in the air between them. "How could you do something like that without talking to me?"

"Because it was the right thing to do. And if we had discussed it beforehand you would have nixed it. Besides, there was no point having this discussion if they weren't coming."

"Oh. My. God. They're coming?"

"Yes."

Ivy pulled her hands from his and shoved them into her hair, grabbing fistfuls of it as she stepped away from Kit. "How could you do something like this without talking to me?" She looked over at him, but he offered no explanation, begged no pardon, just stood unshielded in the storm that was about to break. Ivy's rage was spiraling upward, outward, far beyond her ability to contain it. "How could you do something so inconsiderate? I thought—I thought we were in a partnership. I thought we were in this together?"

She looked at him, wondering how to make him understand the magnitude of his misstep. "I've accepted that we live where we live because it's imperative to your work. I've accepted that the nature of the work you do defines the type of life we can live. I've accepted that Casey and I have to surrender to the dictates of your security concerns, for us, for you, for your team. But within those extreme constraints, I thought—I'd hoped—that you and I would work together on the things we can control. The optional aspects of our life. But I don't even have input into those, do I?"

She shook her head, having a hard time believing he'd done what he had without even discussing it with her. "You know how I feel about my parents. You know that. Why couldn't we have waited a month or two or a year before we dealt with my parents? Why did it have to be now, on a day that means so very much to us, a day you know they will ruin?"

"We don't know they'll ruin it."

"When have they ever not ruined something that had to do with you and me? But that's not even the point of what I'm saying." She paced the width of the patio and back. Looking up at him, she said, "I need to know that you will not be running our lives unilaterally. My father did that, and look how it turned out for them. I need to know I have some say in the elements of our lives that are optional. This was optional."

"No, it wasn't."

"It is. We could have dealt with them at any point in the future. It didn't have to be now."

The patio was lit only by the glow that spilled out from the kitchen and living room, but it was enough to see the look in Kit's eyes. He'd had the same expression so many years ago when the Army and the sheriff had dragged him away from her. It hurt to look at him now, as it had then.

She felt his pain, but did he feel hers?

"We are only ever going to be married once," he said in a quiet voice. "One time, Iv. One time. Your parents have missed all of your adult life. And all of Casey's life. I don't want them to miss this."

Ivy swiped the tears from her cheeks with both hands. "Kit, they're toxic people. They are not good for us or for Casey."

"Maybe so, but they're the only parents we have."

"They aren't parent material. They're not even fit to be called parents. How can you want to bring them here?"

The light caught a spill of moisture on his cheek. Ivy drew a ragged breath.

"I never had parents, Ivy. My dad spawned me and that's it. I was taking care of my mother when I was five. I need your parents, Iv. I *need* them. I want to try to find a way for us to be a family. Please." He blinked. More tears spilled down his cheeks.

"Oh, Kit." Ivy shut her eyes. "I can't do this. It terrifies me."

He wrapped his arms around her and pulled her against his chest. "Me too."

"What if it's a really bad idea? What if they do their typical, hateful nonsense and make problems?"

Kit sniffed. "I gave your father clear guidelines for

the way I expected him to behave. I told him if he couldn't control himself, I'd have his ass on a plane faster than he could blink."

Ivy gasped. "You didn't."

"I did. And I meant it. But we have our side of that bargain to uphold. We have to at least be polite to them. And maybe, just maybe, we can find a way to move forward. As a family."

Ivy sighed. She leaned more fully against him and wrapped her arms around his waist. "Okay. Okay, Kit. We'll make this work. For you, I will do this. But I swear, if they let you down, *I* will have them on a plane so fast."

She drew back and looked up at him. "And now, about our other issue. You're not going to do this again, right? You're not going to make unilateral decisions for us about things that are optional."

"This wasn't optional."

"We disagree on that. But now that I see how important it is to you, I'll make it as important to me. But in the future—"

"In the future, for all things that pertain to us personally, I agree we'll make joint decisions on them. You have my word."

Ivy sighed and leaned against him again. After a minute, she looked up at him and smiled. "So how was it talking to my dad, really?"

Kit grinned. "I used one of Owen's men to deliver the invitation. They're coming out on Owen's jet with a couple more men for the weekend."

Ivy laughed. "Oh my God. I would have loved to have been there."

"I talked to your dad on the phone afterwards. He and I are likely to have words. But we both made it clear that you, Casey, and your mom are to be treated like gold."

"Kit." Ivy shook her head. "This will definitely be a wedding to remember."

"I love you, Iv. I hope we can find a way to make this work with your parents."

Ivy felt fresh tears on her cheeks. Kit deserved this and much more. But there were only so many teeth a person could have kicked out, and her parents had kicked out all of hers and Casey's. She'd be damned if she let them hurt Kit. She had no illusions for how her parents would behave or the prospects of their being a part of their lives in a healthy way. "I'll do my best, Kit, to build that bridge. You have my word on that." She thought of another issue her parents' arrival caused. "What about the sheriff? He was going to walk me down the aisle…"

"I'll talk to him. If things go south with your folks, we'll still need him to do that. Don't worry. He's a cool guy. He'll understand."

CHAPTER FIVE

Glass clinked as Kit pulled a bottle of beer out of the fridge. The girls were having their bachelorette party tonight. In the billiards room. The guys had wanted to take him out, but he didn't want to go. With Ivy's parents coming in tomorrow, he didn't want to be hung over. Besides, Mandy had planned a formal dinner for Ivy and him and the whole team, and Casey was being allowed to attend it, too.

His sister had been running around like a crazy person, getting things ready for tonight. The girls had been secretive and giggly all day. Greer had turned off the cameras and mics in the billiards room—and locked the guys out from turning them back on. None of them knew what the hell was happening in there. He sipped his beer, wondering what dirty things were planned for the adult portion of the night. Greer was absolutely tight-lipped about it. The only thing he'd divulge was that they'd kept within protocol. Which meant they'd gotten any incoming entertainment approved. Or…hell, they were using *Val* to keep things in-house.

Blade and Rocco came into the living room. Blade grabbed a beer; Rocco had his sweet tea. When they sat near him, Kit sent them a pained glare. Blade grinned. "You look like someone's been pulling your short hairs."

Rocco didn't smile. His somber gaze settled on Kit. "You sure about all this? Getting married?"

"It's the one thing I'm absolutely certain of. How about you? Things with my sis going okay?"

"They are."

He caught Rocco's stillness and frowned. "You gonna give her your name soon?"

Rocco made a face. "I did that once. Totally fucked someone's life."

"That wasn't a real marriage," Kit countered.

"It was to her."

"Yeah? Then why'd she try to kill your ass? And Zavi, too?"

Blade held up a hand as his gaze sliced toward Kit. "Not tonight. Tonight's for mischief. Rocco doesn't need to rush into anything. Unlike you, pining for Ivy since I met you."

Rocco ignored that attempted redirection. "Has Mandy said something to you?"

"No. She's happy, man. Happier than I've ever seen. You're good for her. And I think she's good for you." He sipped his beer. "I got a favor to ask you guys."

"Anything," Blade answered without hesitation.

"Help me contain Val tonight. I gotta tie him up and lock him in somewhere."

"Too bad my old cage is gone. Finally have a legit use for it."

Kit was surprised Blade could joke about something that still haunted him. He set his bottle down on the coffee table and stood up. "Let's go."

"Where?" Rocco asked.

"Have a talk with Val."

They went upstairs and down the hallway. They passed Fiona's and Eden's rooms. They were together in Fee's room—the men could hear laughter as they went past. Kit shared a look with the others, his mood becoming almost as dour as Rocco's. In the southern wing, he knocked on Val's door. There was movement inside the room. After a minute, the door opened.

Val stood there shirtless in low-rise jeans. Jesus, the guy was ripped. "'Sup?" Val asked.

Kit pushed inside his room. Rocco and Blade followed him, closing the door behind them. Clothes were tossed all over the bed as if the pretty boy couldn't pick just one outfit. "Goin' somewhere?" Kit asked as he plopped himself down on Val's bed, on top of the clothes, and leaned against the headboard.

"Yeah. Your bachelor party. Hold on. Let me finish getting dressed." Going over to his dresser, he picked up a black bow tie and fastened it around his neck. "I'm ready."

"What the hell, Val? Why would you do something like that? I don't want to look at you," Kit snarled.

Val grinned. "We're crashing the girls' gig."

"No, we're not." Rocco tucked his hands under his armpits and spread his legs.

"Oh yes we are. They have *costumes*."

"What kind of costumes?" Kit asked.

"No idea. They picked them out when we went shopping. Somebody"—he gave Kit the evil eye—"wouldn't let me in the dressing rooms. Didn't you see what Ivy brought home?"

"No. She put her stuff in my old room and wouldn't let me go in there."

"How about you guys?" Val asked the other two.

Rocco and Blade looked at each other. "No."

"And you call yourselves Red Teamers. You're a disgrace to the unit."

Blade grinned. "So what's the plan?"

Val held up a couple decks of cards. "We lie low until things heat up. When they send Casey out, we'll know things are about to get serious. We let 'em drink, get rowdy. Then we crash it, when their resistance is down and they need some testosterone."

"Just one problem with that plan. Have you talked to Greer?" Kit asked.

"No."

"Then how do you know they don't have the testosterone end of things covered with a few hired strippers?"

"That ain't happening," Rocco growled.

Kit's glare went his way. "What do you think all the giggling's about?"

"It's cool." Blade's smile wasn't quite a smile. "The only way in for their entertainment's through the front door. And us."

"So we wait." Kit got off the bed. He picked up a black tee shirt and tossed it toward Val. "And cover up. I don't need to see man-nips all night."

Val pulled the tee on. Kit frowned when he saw that it didn't quite hit the waistband of his low jeans, leaving a thin strip of skin to showcase his obliques. He slipped on a pair of flip-flops then held his hands out to show he was ready.

"Lose the bow," Kit ordered.

Val pulled it off and slipped it into a pocket. "We could have brought in our own strippers and spared ourselves the torture of deprivation—and the need to crash their party, you know."

"Who needs strippers when we've got the real deal?" Blade asked as he opened the door.

"One-third of the team is taken care of, but the other two-thirds aren't. And you're not sharing. Would it hurt you to at least let me get—or give—a lap dance?"

"Nope. Wouldn't hurt me a bit." Kit smiled. "But it would kill you."

* * *

Kit looked up when Greer's phone rang. The girls had been moving back and forth down the hall, lowering their conversations to hushed whispers when they passed in front of the living room. Kathy and Dennis had blocked off the dining room after lunch, moving the two large screens in front of the wide entrance into the living room. Dinner was being served later than usual. Kathy was feeding Zavi in the kitchen and Dennis was going to babysit him until Rocco and Mandy went to bed.

"Copy that," Greer said, then hung up. The entire team was in the living room. Greer's call hadn't come from one of the guys.

"What's doin', Greer?" Kit asked.

"Nothing." He set his beer down then tapped something on his phone, dimming the lights in the living room. "We got incoming."

"Incoming what?" Owen asked.

"Women."

Kit narrowed his eyes. "What kind of women?"

"From the eighteenth century, I'd say. And, before you kick my ass, all protocols were followed. Just for the record."

The screens were pulled back from the dining room, revealing the long table shimmering in a white damask tablecloth with gold and white dishes, lit candelabras, pastel flower bouquets. Kit looked at Blade, wondering where the hell the fancy dishes came from. Blade just shrugged.

He heard a growing commotion in the hallway. When he looked that way, women were spilling into the room, lots of them, dressed in uber short, poufy skirts, laced-up bodices, thigh-high stockings, high heels. They wore tall white wigs that made Marge Simpson's hair look tame. And ornate masks. He couldn't tell who was who at first—nine of them and one very small woman. The little one came and stood in front of him, grinning up at him.

Casey.

In that absurd getup, she looked older than her twelve years, though, granted, her heels weren't as high, nor her skirt as short as the adult women, who were now weaving their way among the men. Kit searched the room for Ivy, trying to calm his rage. Trying not to look at the rich array of breasts mounded above tight bustiers or the flashes of bare thighs exposed by the short skirts and thigh-high stockings.

Two women touched him and laughed, leaning against him before flitting away. His body was tightening. He could feel himself hardening at just the thought that one of these women was his Ivy. He looked around the room at the other guys, seeing they were all standing like wary statues. Except for Val, who was grinning like a child on Christmas morning. As Kit watched, he wrapped an arm around Greer's neck and kissed his face. "I freaking love you, man."

"Don't thank me. This was all the girls' idea." Greer looked over at Kit. "I just followed the protocol."

The fucking protocol needed an update.

"Isn't it fun, Dad? It was so hard to keep it a secret from you."

"I don't like secrets, Casey."

"But you like this one."

Before he could answer, Ivy was there. He knew her first by scent, then by the feel of her arm in his, the heat of her body. "Case—go grab a Coke from the bar," he said, sending her away so that he could speak with Ivy. "She's a kid, Iv."

"Yes. She is. And she'll head to her room after supper. She has a couple of movies to watch."

He looked around the room. "Who are these women?"

"Mandy, Eden, and Fiona, plus a few friends who were excited to spend an evening with your single teammates. After supper, we'll leave you in peace and head down to the billiards room." He wasn't happy. She gave him that look. He could see it even through the mask. "Kit, it's a masquerade, not an orgy. Chill."

He looked down at the soft mounds of her breasts. He didn't want to chill. He wanted her on his lap, wanted to watch her eyes through that mask while he slipped inside of her, wanted to bang her in that ridiculous outfit—

"I put some cherries in my Coke. Is that okay, Dad?" Casey asked as she rejoined them. Kit blinked down at her, but couldn't find the words to answer her.

"It's fine, sweetheart," Ivy answered for him. "I see Kathy waving us in to dinner. Let's go have a seat."

Kit caught Ivy up against him before she'd taken a step. "You're staying in that outfit after your party, feel me?"

She drew a long breath through red-painted lips. "Oh, I do. Did I tell you I'm not wearing anything under this?" she asked in a whisper.

He pulled her in tighter and bent to kiss her bare shoulder. "Fuck dinner," he growled against her skin. "I can't even move after seeing you in this."

She laughed and pushed against him. "We've guests. Behave."

Kit took his designated seat at the full dining table. Casey sat between him and Ivy. The women were vivacious, filling the room with the soft sounds of their voices and laughter. Kelan, Rocco, and Blade were quiet and often unable to tear their eyes from their women. Greer, Val, and Angel were charming the hell out of the women nearest them. Max was absent—Kit hoped he'd be able to make it back for the wedding. Owen was his usual somber self, but Kit didn't miss his brooding glances down the table…toward Selena. Kit wondered if Owen was second-guessing bringing her onto the team.

When the meal was over, the group lingered in the living room. The girls were congregating around Val, Angel, and Greer. Eden and Fiona were with their guys and Owen at the bar. Rocco retrieved Zavi from the kitchen and took him over to kiss Mandy good night.

"Case—Zavi and I are going to watch some movies, want to join us?" Rocco asked.

"Sure. What movies did you get? I have some, too."

He called off a few titles from movie franchises Kit didn't recognize.

"I'm picking the first movie," Zavi said.

"Okay. I'll pick the second one." Casey gave Kit a hug, then kissed Ivy. "I wish I could stay with you, Mom."

"I know. But it's grown-up time. I'll tell you all about it in the morning—but not too early! I might need to sleep in tomorrow. Good night, sweetheart."

Kit looked over at Rocco, silently reminding him they had plans for the night.

"Thought I'd give Dennis a break. I'll be back after they crash," Rocco told him as he lifted Zavi to his shoulders.

* * *

Rocco and the kids walked down the hall that led to the north wing. His suite was right above Kit's. He paused at the stairs. "Get in your PJs," he told Casey, "and do your teeth, then come up and join us."

"Can't I stay in my costume?"

"You could. But you might be more comfortable in pajamas. Besides, Kathy's bringing us a treat she sneaked out of the party. You don't want to get that outfit dirty."

"Okay. I'll be right up, Uncle Rocco."

A few minutes later, with Zavi tucked against his side on the sofa, Rocco started the movie previews. Casey came upstairs, then quietly started down the hallway to the bridge overlooking the main living room, creeping forward slowly so she wouldn't be spotted.

"Case, come on back here. Let the adults have their time."

She returned to the sitting room. Zavi was leaning over a tray of cocoa mugs and a selection of *petit fours* and stunning cupcakes. "Oh, those are beautiful. Which one are you having, Zavi?"

"Pink is for girls. I don't like pink."

Casey laughed. "There are some yellow ones, or you can have the chocolate one."

He took a chocolate cupcake then settled back against Rocco. Casey put a couple of goodies on a plate then sat on Rocco's other side. She didn't eat immediately, just stared at the plate.

"What's up, Case?" Rocco asked. The movie had started and Zavi was thoroughly absorbed in the cartoon characters.

"I helped decorate the party room. It was beautiful," she told him.

"I bet it was."

"Everything's going to be okay, right, Uncle Rocco?"

Rocco didn't immediately answer. He couldn't. He'd been wondering the same thing. He blinked. What she feared wasn't at all what he feared; they were talking about her, not him. "What's worrying you?"

"My grandparents are coming tomorrow. My mom hates them. They hate my dad. And me."

Man, he wished she weren't laying this on him. Not now. It was a convo she needed to have with her parents. He looked down the hall, considered grabbing Kit and letting the two of them talk things out. But Kit was neck deep in fun.

And she'd come to him.

It was such a weight for her slim shoulders to carry. "Listen, baby. Sometimes life doesn't go quite as planned. People screw up. Sometimes…sometimes it's just nice to start over. Think of it this way. What's the worst thing you've ever done?" Probably a stupid analogy. She was too young to be haunted by her choices.

"I told my mom I hated her once. But I don't. I wish I hadn't said that."

"Wouldn't it be nice if you could have a do-over? Make that mistake go away? Forgive yourself for saying that, and forgive your mom for whatever it was she did that made you so angry with her, and just start again?"

"That would be nice."

"Maybe that's what'll happen this weekend with your grandparents. Maybe you'll find they want a new start. Maybe you should give them that chance."

"Does that work for everyone?"

He looked at her, feeling the shadows press in against him. He wished it did. "Not always."

She still studied her plate of treats, then set it aside and turned toward him, tucking her feet beneath his thigh.

"But, why, Uncle Rocco? I just don't get it. Why would they hate my mom?"

Rocco looked down at her, into her big blue eyes. Like he had any fucking answers for anything at all relating to humans. Or life. Or reality. He looked away. Maybe he could ignore her question, ignore her fragile belief in humanity before he crushed her innocence and told her the truth. Life was fucked up and she should quit believing in sweetness and light, because that was a fast road to madness.

"Life isn't fair, Case. And most of the time it doesn't make a whole lot of sense. Let's just watch the movie. Tomorrow will resolve itself."

CHAPTER SIX

"You girls need a bartender?" Val asked the females in the room as they were leaving for the billiards room.

"Yes!" one of the costumed women answered. Kit recognized her voice as that of the waitress from Winchester's. "Fee, please. We need a man thing in there with us."

"No," Kelan answered for the men.

Fiona laughed. "It's up to Mandy. She organized everything."

Mandy deferred to Ivy. Before Ivy could answer, Val pulled off his tee and was snapping that damned bow tie around his neck. He looked at her and held out his hands, ever the irrepressible sex-bot. "I'll stay behind the bar."

"He'll divulge all of our secrets to the guys," Ivy warned.

"Nope. They won't get a word out of me," he vowed.

"What secrets?" Kit asked.

"Nothing," Ivy answered, but she couldn't hide her smile. "Fine. He can come. But give Kit your phone." Val handed it over. "And your earpiece."

"Not wearing one."

"And any other listening or watching device."

He held up his hands. "I'm clean."

"Make him pinky swear to keep our secrets secret," Fee suggested.

Val held up his pinky and hooked it around Ivy's. "I pinky swear that what happens at your bridal shower, stays in the shower."

Ivy laughed. "That didn't sound right."

"You gonna let him do this?" Kelan asked, frowning at Kit.

He shrugged. "It's their party. He knows his boundaries." The girls started to file out of the living room. "Besides, we're gonna crash it in a little while. We need someone on the inside to let us in." Kelan didn't look convinced. "Relax. The girls are with Fee. Nothing's going to happen."

"Ivy." Greer stopped her before she stepped into the hallway. "You've got the room for two hours. After that, you turn into pumpkins, the lockdown releases, and these yahoos can see what you're doing."

Ivy grinned and waved to him. "Thanks, Greer. Love you, Kit!" She blew him a kiss.

The guys settled down to an uneasy game of

poker. Kit tried to focus on the game for a few hands, but his ears were straining for sounds of the party. He looked at his watch. For the hundredth time. Five more minutes had passed. When the next hand held useless cards, he folded.

He grabbed a beer, then leaned against the bar and watched the guys. Blade looked up at him, then back at his cards. "Greer, you know this is Kit's bachelor party."

"Yep."

"Unlock the game room. Let us at least see what's goin' on in there. Kit needs some entertainment."

"No can do." Greer didn't look up from his cards. "I gave my word. Ivy entered her own password for the room. Don't know what it is."

"Bullshit. You've got an override," Blade growled.

Greer laid down his cards, winning the hand with an ace-high straight. "So I do."

"Leave them be." Kit sipped his beer. "I'm grateful they had the party here. Made logistics easier. Besides, they only have an hour and twenty minutes remaining."

"Is Max coming in for the wedding?" Angel asked, looking from Kit to Owen. Kit thought about Max, deep undercover with the White Kingdom Brotherhood motorcycle gang. His absence was the only shadow over Kit's joy this weekend. Well, that and his worries about Ivy's parents.

"He knows about it. He'll be here if he can," Greer answered.

A door down the hallway banged open. Female laughter spilled into the hallway, pooling in the living room. Tension lifted the hairs on Kit's arms as a pair of high-heeled shoes clicked on the hardwood floor, heading this way. One of the women appeared at the entrance to the living room. All the men looked at her. Her gaze swept the room and settled on Kelan. She ran to him, sat on his lap, and assaulted his mouth with her own. K's arms wrapped around her, bringing her tighter as he deepened the kiss. Watching them make out, Kit felt heat pool in his groin. After a minute, Fee pulled back and snapped a selfie of her on K's lap.

"Fiona—" Kelan complained.

"It was a dare. I didn't want to answer the question, so I had to kiss the closest man." She bit her bottom lip then added, "You were the only man I saw." She kissed his nose, hopped off his lap, and ran out of the living room, lipstick smeared across her mouth.

"Uh, K?" Blade made a motion with his finger, indicating the smeared lipstick she'd left on him.

Kelan dragged the back of his fist across his lips, slowly, as if breathing in the scent of her lipstick. Kit set his empty beer on the bar and crossed his arms, wondering what more tortures the girls would send their way. He didn't have to wait long. Another woman came into the room. Kit didn't recognize her, so she had to be one of the friends the girls had brought in. She scanned the room.

Owen was behind the bar, getting a bottle of his Balcones. When the girl saw him, she headed in his direction, slipping behind the bar to stand in front of him. He frowned down at her, giving her the look that made grown men stutter. The girl reached a hand to his shoulder, then retracted it before making contact. The awkwardness of her indecision stretched the moment thin before she pivoted and hurried out of the room.

Owen shook his head. He'd no sooner retrieved a glass than another of the females came into the living room and made a beeline for him. He ignored her while he poured his drink. Lifting the glass to his lips, he casually looked at the girl over the rim. Kit actually felt sorry for her; he'd gotten a similar glare when he'd fucked something up on a mission. The girl gave him a silly smile and waved at him as if it had been her intent to merely stand within three feet of him and survive. She turned away and walked quickly out of the room.

Owen caught Kit's amused look and narrowed his eyes. He topped off his drink, then started toward the end of the bar. He didn't get any farther before a third woman marched into the room, followed by Selena. The newest member of the team stayed in the foyer, watching the proceedings with a Mona Lisa smile. Owen ignored the girl coming toward him as his gaze locked on to Selena's. After a second, he looked down at the girl offering herself to him.

He slammed his glass on the bar. "What's it gonna

be? A kiss? A fuck? Your call. Right here. Right now."

In a haze of alcohol-induced courage, the girl stepped toward him, reaching an arm around his shoulder. Owen hooked a hand around her neck and drew her in close, bending to touch his mouth to hers, maneuvering her jaw open for full tongue contact. His arms tightened around her, lifting her against himself, grinding against her until she moaned. His eyes opened. He looked over at Selena, even as his tongue was busy with the woman in his arms.

Selena's smile slowly died, replaced by that same hard-edged look she'd given Amir Hadad when she'd caught him here in the house. If the kiss went on much longer, Owen was going to be gutted, Kit thought. Owen released the girl, but spared not so much as a look at her. His gaze never left Selena. The girl stumbled back a step, then sent Owen an appreciative smile. Before she could move back into his arms, Selena came forward and grabbed her arm, leading her out of the room.

"I told you I could do it," the girl boasted as they went into the hallway.

Kit turned and looked over at Blade and the others, wondering if they'd seen what had just transpired. All of the guys looked at him, then quickly resumed their card game. Kit checked his watch. A half-hour to go before the pumpkins opened the room. Jesus. Some weird shit was going on in there.

"That's it," Owen snapped. He threw back the rest of his Balcones, then slammed the glass on the counter and started for the hall.

"What are you doing, Owen?"

"It's time to rout the pumpkins."

"No. No, it is not." Kit followed him out of the living room, sending a look back at the others for backup.

"They can't keep sending females out to assault us." The door to the game room was locked. "Greer, open it." He stepped back and looked at the IT guy.

"Can't do it, boss. They have twenty more minutes."

"They have no more minutes. Override it. Now."

The door opened and one of the wigged women came out. She hesitated, her gaze bouncing from man to man before a red flush overtook her face. "Excuse me—I was just headed to the powder room." She pointed to the bathroom across the hall. The guys parted, letting her through. Someone came over to close the door, but Owen put his foot in the opening and pushed inside.

Kit and the others followed him into the room but came to an abrupt stop a few feet inside. Piles of lingerie were draped over the leather sofa and side tables, sexy bits of lace and silk spilling out of boxes. It looked like an orgy was taking place in the middle of the room. Three women, still in their costumes, were tangled on a section of the carpet, bordered on two sides by the other women. Folded paper tents marked rows of the foot-long squares in the checkered carpet as Green, Yellow, Blue, Red. Two other women were holding cards. One called off a color, one a left or right foot or hand.

Twister. Not an orgy. When the girls became aware of the guys, they crumpled into a giggling heap. Angel and Greer went over to help untangle them.

"What the hell are you guys doin'?" Val hissed from behind the bar counter. From where he stood, he'd had a perfect view of the women in their compromising poses. "They have the room for another half-hour or so." He leaned over the counter and lowered his voice as he explained, "Things were just getting good. They accept a dare when they step onto the board. The first who falls has to execute the challenge."

Kit made a face. "Your idea?"

"Oh yeah. And believe me, I am the beneficiary of their enthusiasm."

"Mm-hmm. You and Owen," Kit snapped.

"It's far less scandalous than what was going on over there. 'Pin the Peen on Kit' and 'Ivy's Dildo Toss.'"

"*What?*"

The girls from the makeshift Twister board were dragging the guys over to the other side of the room. A life-sized poster of a man holding a target over his privates had been taped to the wall. Where the man's face should have been, a color printout of Kit's face was. Taped in the vicinity of his groin were a variety of pseudo penises: a cartoon of a large carrot and two tomatoes, a twisting snake, a bent penis, and a dozen other cardboard phallic images.

Two soft arms slipped around Kit's waist as Ivy's sweet scent drifted up to him. He sighed. "Really? This?" he asked as he turned to face her.

She smiled. "You should have heard the commentary when the girls were attaching your parts. Thank God the audio was off." She looked at him through a frown. "It was off, wasn't it?"

"It was off."

"I'm glad the guys came in. They're really why the girls came over tonight."

"Yeah, we're not playthings, Ivy," Owen complained as he leaned against the bar.

"Seriously, O?" Val asked as he set some glasses out on the bar. "I sent girls to you, and you chased them away. How much easier could I make it for you?"

"How about letting me pick my own?"

Val shrugged. "Whatevs. Seemed you were having trouble in that area." He poured a whiskey and pushed it toward Owen.

Angel and Greer had collected the plastic rings and were tossing them over the blow-up penis, receiving a kiss from one of the girls with each successful toss, which was every toss for them.

"Guys, that's just wrong," Kit called over to them.

Angel shrugged. "When in Rome, my friend…"

One of the girls stepped behind the bar and came up to Val, rubbing her hand up and down his arm. He smiled at her as he lifted her to sit on the counter next to the sink. "There something I can get you?" he asked.

"Yes." She hooked her arms around his neck. "You've been serving everyone except me."

Val grinned and bent down as if to kiss her, but on the way, Selena snagged his gaze. He paused then straightened. His nostrils flared as his expression hardened. Owen shifted, intercepting his gaze. The two men stared at each other for a long moment before Val returned his attention to the bargirl from Winchester's. He didn't look at Selena again. Instead, he dipped his head and latched on to the woman's mouth, swallowing her next giggle. Selena walked away from the bar and went over to the pool table to set up a game. Owen trailed after her as Val and the girl stepped out of the room.

Kit plopped down on one of the stools in front of the bar as he considered all of the night's strangeness. When Ivy pushed between his legs and lifted her arms to his shoulders, his focus shifted to her. She'd ditched the gilded mask. He loved looking into her eyes, but he had plans for that mask.

"Kit, this is my wedding shower and our bachelor-bachelorette party. Can you believe it? This is really happening."

He smiled. "Just hit you, huh?"

She nodded. "For years, I dreamed about this. When you were in my heart, I never felt alone." She blinked, as if lost in those memories. "And then I gave up on us. I was never so empty as I was when I thought we'd never be together again. When you came back, I was so scared. I didn't want the hurt of losing you again."

"Iv, it's done." He touched her face. "That's in the past. From here out, we move forward together."

"Are you happy?"

"There are no words for the joy I'm feeling right now." He looked at the improvised art taped to the wall. "And I'm sorta creeped out."

She laughed. He loved that sound. "Where's Rocco?" she asked.

Kit sent a look around the room. "He was watching a movie with the kids. Said he'd join us when they crashed." He stood up. "Let's go look for him. Grab your mask."

"Why do I need my mask?"

Kit grinned. "You don't. I do."

CHAPTER SEVEN

Ivy fetched her mask, then Kit took her hand and led her out of the room and down the hallway. As they neared the kitchen, he could hear the soundtrack of a kid's flick playing from the upstairs hallway. He stepped into the temperature-controlled wine cellar and flipped the light on. He made a quick adjustment on his phone to lock the doors and interrupt the security system. The slender room could be entered from either the main hallway or butler's hallway between the dining room and kitchen—he didn't want to run the risk of being interrupted.

"It's cold in here," she whispered.

"Not for long." He lifted her to the butcher-block table. "Put your mask on." He ran a hand up her leg, feeling the shift from elastic lace at the top of her stocking to the smooth, silky skin of her bare thigh. He pushed his hand up her skirt, moving up the length of her leg to her bottom. He started to suck in a harsh breath as his hand met only bare skin, but his fingertips hit the strap of her thong.

"You lied," he growled.

She leaned back, supporting herself on her palms. "About what?"

"About being bare-assed."

"A thong isn't much cover."

"It's more than I want right now." He hooked his fingers in the edge of her panties and pulled down. She lifted her hips so he could draw them all the way off. They got tangled at her shoes. She didn't help him, other than to point her toes. When he looked up at her, he saw she'd put her mask back on. She ran her teeth over her lip. His cock jerked in reaction. His grip tightened on her ankle. "Iv, don't fuck with me right now. I haven't been able to think of anything except being in you since I first saw you in this getup."

She put her foot on his waist, catching his belt under her heel. "Take yourself out. Let's see how worked up you are."

He undid his fly and reached inside, adjusting his clothes to let himself out. His cock was as hard as a marble dildo.

"All of you. Your balls too."

"Iv—"

"Do it."

Kit clenched his teeth as he cupped his balls, pulling himself forward. His dick pointed straight ahead, perfectly angled toward the shadows of her short skirt. She leaned forward and grasped him in her soft hands. Her touch made him throb. He breathed through the pain of wanting her. Still holding him in one hand, she cupped his cheek in her other hand and touched her soft lips to his.

He took hold of her face, owning the kiss, fucking her mouth with his tongue as she stroked his rigid length below. Easing a hand from her face, he set it on her leg and pushed it up beneath her skirt, finding the juncture of her legs and the narrow strip of curls hidden there. He pushed his fingers between her folds, up and back, spending time at the top of her sex, feeling it thicken.

Taking hold of her ass, he drew her forward to the edge of the table, then stroked her with the blunt head of his cock. Her hands tightened on his shoulders as she looked down to watch him enter her. Her skirts hid what she wanted to see. She lifted them away as he slipped inside her. She sucked in a ragged breath as he withdrew, then shoved in again. He reached into her bodice and cupped a breast, bending over her to taste the soft skin where her neck and shoulder met.

Shit. He hadn't covered himself. Still deep inside of her, he held still. "Iv, I need a rubber."

"No. You don't."

"Honey, you ready for that?"

She lifted his face and smiled into his eyes. "I've never been more ready for anything in my life. You are a wonderful dad. It's time we grew our family."

"I know nothing about being a father."

"Then you have phenomenal instincts. Look at Casey. She adores you. You always keep a balance of fun and expectations."

Kit hissed a long breath as he leaned his forehead against hers, holding himself still. His dick throbbed in complaint. "Mid-fuck is so not the time to decide something like this."

"If you're not ready to grow our family, put a rubber on. But I'm ready. More than ready. To have your child again. To have you near me the whole time. To have you be with me for every significant event."

"That's something I may not be able to do—be here for every event."

"You know what I mean. We're together. We're a family. I don't have to do any of this alone. You don't have to miss any of it. And if you are absent, because work sends you away, I'll fill you in. Our lives are one now."

He ran his hand up her back, reaching up to hold her neck as he shoved into her. He kissed her mouth. His breathing was as ragged as hers. "I love you, Ivy. The life you're laying out is all I've ever wanted. To belong somewhere, to someone. To be wanted. Needed."

"I do need you, Kit."

"Forever."

"Forever."

"Even when we're old and have grandchildren?"

"Especially then."

"Even when our kids and grandkids do something boneheaded like have a kid?" he asked.

"Whatever comes. We'll face it as a family."

"Even when I do something thoughtless like inviting your parents without telling you?"

"Even when you make me furious. I adore you."

"Only me…"

"Only you."

He kissed her, letting his tongue play with hers. His thrusts grew more rapid, but he didn't want to rush this, and Christ, he was close. He reached down and lifted her legs, raising them to put her ankles on his shoulders. She leaned back to accommodate their new position. He took hold of her hips and banged into her.

He reached over to put a hand on her flat belly, imagining his child growing there. "Iv, take off your mask. I want to see your face when you come."

He fingered her clit as she removed the glittery cover. Her lips parted. A little frown drew a line between her brows. Her nostrils flared. He could feel her inner muscles contract, grabbing his cock. God, he couldn't hold on much longer. She cried out when she went over the edge, her hips shivering against his. He palmed her ass, slamming into her, thrusting against the clamp of her channel. When his release came, she peaked again.

When their bodies calmed, he eased her legs down

his arms, then helped her sit up. She wrapped her arms around his chest, in no hurry to go anywhere. Nor was he. In her arms was right where he wanted to be. They stayed that way for a few minutes before he put himself back together.

"Hey. Do you want to ditch the wig and put some jeans on before we go back?" He bent down and retrieved her panties, but shoved them in his pocket instead of giving them back to her.

"Good call." She slipped off the table and straightened her short, puffy skirt.

Kit reset the security in the small room, then walked Ivy down to their room. He went to the window and drew the curtains, then sat in one of the armchairs and observed as she removed her wig and costume. She pulled on a fresh pair of lace panties then brushed out her hair. He was getting a hard-on watching her. He had to adjust himself when she pulled a pair of jeans up her lean legs.

She looked over at him. He smiled. "You have a beautiful body."

"Will you say that when I'm out to here with a baby?" she asked, stretching her hands in front of her.

"I'll say that every day for the rest of our lives."

She strolled over to sit on his lap and hug him. "I wish we hadn't lost so much time."

He took hold of her face and kissed her cheek, her eye, her temple. "Don't look back, Iv. Just be here now. With me. Forever."

She nodded. He felt the sweep of her eyelash. "I

love you."

"I love you." His words spilled across her cheek. He was considering talking her into staying where they were, but before he'd settled on a tactic, she got off his lap. He squelched his request. It wasn't right for him to keep her hidden here alone with him. He watched her take a couple of loose tees from her drawer. She pulled one, then the other, over her head. A quick stop in the bathroom, then she was ready.

"I need to check in on Case and Rocco before we go back. You mind?" he asked.

"Not at all."

He took her hand and led her out of their room and into Casey's. Their daughter was sound asleep in her bed. Kit remembered how much of an outsider he'd felt when she and Ivy first came to live here. He'd been standing on the outside looking in at everything he'd ever wanted in his life. Now they were his. He looked over at Ivy, wondering if she understood how much the two of them meant to him.

She wasn't looking at Casey. She was watching him. "You look like you just came home," she whispered.

He pulled her into his arms. "I never had a home before, until you and Case."

"The same goes for us, Kit." She nestled more deeply into his arms. He loved the feel of her against his body. After a minute, they moved quietly out of Casey's room and went upstairs. A DVD was playing a looping run of initial screens on the TV in Rocco's sitting room, but no one was watching it. Kit shut it off, then knocked on Rocco's door.

No answer.

He looked back at Ivy, then had her wait in the sitting room while he went into Rocco's room. It was empty. He went next door into Zavi's room. Rocco's son was sleeping peacefully, a tiny person in the extra-long twin bed. He went back to the sitting room and called Rocco's phone.

No answer. He called Greer. "You're missing a helluva party, boss," Greer answered.

"My bad. We'll be there shortly. Where's Rocco?"

"Hold on." Greer went silent, then came back on the line. "He's parked on the patio outside the kitchen."

"Okay."

"Need something?"

"Nope. Thanks." He hung up the phone. "Iv—"

She smiled and leaned up to kiss his cheek. "Don't worry. I'll head back to the party. Take your time. Let me know if you need me or Mandy."

* * *

A wide portico ran the length of the back of the house. It could be accessed by all of the rooms from the den all the way down to the south bedroom wing. Mosquito torches were lit midway outside the room where Ivy's bachelorette party was being held. Here, by the kitchen, there were only shadows.

And Rocco, who sat on the steps leading down to the lawn.

Kit went over and sat next to him. He listened in silence to the crickets. Now and then, hunting calls of a pair of owls rolled across the empty space. The torchlights attracted insects, and the insects attracted bats, but their hunter-prey dance was entirely silent.

"What's doin', Rocco?"

He wasn't quick to answer. "It a crime to sit outside at night?"

"Crime? No. Curious? Yes. Especially when there's a party going on that your girlfriend's hosting."

More long moments of silence, then Rocco stood up. "Wouldn't want to miss the fun."

Kit slowly came to his feet, standing in Rocco's space, blocking him. "What's with the attitude?"

Rocco stared at him in the dark light of the yard. "You think I got a problem? I don't. Ain't a single fucking thing wrong. I have my son back. I have a woman men would start wars over. I have a job I enjoy. What makes you think I have a problem?"

"I don't think you have a problem. I think you got devils. I think you need help working through them. You aren't alone, Rocco. Blade and I are here for you now, like we have been all along."

Rocco shrugged then shoved a hand through his hair. "Forget it. I'm fine. I just get a little stir crazy when things are too quiet." He stepped around Kit and started for the party at the opposite end of the long patio.

Kit shoved his hands in his pockets and followed him. When his feet stepped into the pool of light spilling from the billiards room, he forced himself to relax his shoulders and hide the tension he felt. He and Rocco were met with the perceptive eyes of his sister and Ivy. He smiled to reassure them all was well.

But it was not A-okay for Rocco. Far from it.

CHAPTER EIGHT

Ivy's nose came awake first, roused by the rich scent of coffee in the mugs Kit brought with him into their room. She propped an eye open and saw the bright light of day the heavy drapes tried to block. She shoved herself up to look at the clock. "Oh, God! What time is it?"

Kit sat on the bed. He wore jeans, but otherwise was barefoot and shirtless. "Take it easy, Iv. You're not late for anything. Val said you girls weren't due at the hair salon until noon. And your parents won't be here before this afternoon."

She looked at Kit, giving her mind time to finish waking up. She shoved her hair out of her face, glad to realize she hadn't had so much to drink the night before that she was uncomfortable now. She pulled herself to a sitting position and leaned back against the headboard. Kit handed her a mug. She cupped her hands around it and lifted it to her nose to breathe in the antidote to last night's excesses.

"Where is everyone?" she asked, venturing a sip of the steaming liquid.

"Casey's with Zavi and Mandy, taking care of the horses. Angel and Val have taken the women home. Fee and Eden are cleaning up the billiards room."

"Why didn't they wake me earlier? I could have helped them."

"I thought it best, given that it's D-Day, that you got as much rest as possible."

She sipped the coffee again. "Kit, I'm fine. I'm a grown-up. You don't have to tiptoe around me. Yes, my parents are coming. I'm sort of looking forward to seeing them, now that I've gotten used to the idea." She reached over and held his hand. "I trust you. If they're vile, evil, terrible people, you'll vanquish them. And if they're essentially nice people who screwed up, we'll figure things out."

Kit smiled and leaned over to kiss her forehead. "That's my girl." He settled next to her and wrapped his arm around her shoulders, drawing her close to him. "So you're not worried about meeting them?"

She shook her head. "I've been giving it a lot of thought. I'm scared to death. But I know you'll make it right. One way or another, it'll work out."

"Kelan's shaman has arrived, Dan Broken Knife. He agrees with K the place is toxic. Blade and Kelan are helping him get settled. He's going to be starting immediately. It's a big job. He wants to get the house cleared before tomorrow night so that he can treat us and prepare the space for our wedding ceremony."

Ivy looked up at Kit. "What do you think of him? Is he the real deal?"

"He's an interesting guy. Owen's pretty skeptical of the whole process. In my mind, anything that helps Blade heal from the shit that went down here as a kid, and anything that helps us get started on the right foot, well, it just can't be all that bad."

"It was a nice gift from Kelan." She took a last swallow of coffee then threw off the covers. "I have so much to do today. But first, a shower." She took his hand and got off the bed, towing him along behind her.

* * *

The house was unusually quiet, Ty thought. Val and Angel were seeing the girls back to their cars. Kit was with Ivy. The other guys were in the bunker. Kathy and Carla were in the kitchen, talking softly. He didn't know where the rest of the women were.

He and Kelan were with Dan Broken Knife and his assistants. The shaman wanted to start his work in the basement. Interesting choice, Ty thought. He wondered if Kelan had given him the history of the house. Ty watched the basement door as they approached, breathing through the tightness clamping his stomach. It was a door. Then stairs. Then the whole fucking basement. Lots of houses had them.

Concrete walls and windows. There was nothing down there. Not anymore.

Kelan put a hand on his shoulder. He looked over at his friend, realizing they'd been standing outside the door longer than he'd intended. Ty's gaze bounced from Kelan to Dan and his two assistants. None of them seemed in a hurry, nor were they concerned at the delay.

"Kelan," Dan said without taking his eyes from Ty, "your friend and I will go down alone at first. You will wait for us here."

Ty opened the door and stepped onto the wooden landing. He didn't pause, didn't wait to be sure Dan was behind him. He went down the stairs and moved to the back of the house where the window wells let in the morning sunlight. Dan followed him down. He looked at Ty, then walked to the opposite side where the cage had been.

The bars had been removed and the steel ends had been dug out of the concrete. The excavation had left deep tracks in the foundation that had been filled in with freshly poured concrete, making a rectangular scar in the floor, a ghost outline of the cage. Dan lifted his hands and mumbled something unintelligible. After a minute, he walked the entire perimeter of the basement, feeling the air with his hands, murmuring into the space.

The shaman came back to stand in front of Ty. He was a middle-aged Indian with twin braids wrapped in crisscrossing strips of red rawhide that hung in front of his shoulders. He had a deep, barrel chest and wore a natural cotton tunic shirt that was heavily beaded around the neck, over the shoulders, and down the arms. Hanging from his ears were silver earrings that looked like elongated teardrops. A large squash blossom necklace of silver and turquoise hung about his neck. Several heavy silver and turquoise cuffs covered his wrists. On one hand was a heavy silver ring with a design Ty couldn't quite make out. His black eyes were never evasive. They were, in fact, uncomfortably perceptive. Ty forced himself not to look away.

"We'll go back upstairs now and prepare for the ceremony." He gestured toward the stairs, then followed Ty up. Once in the hallway, he spoke to his assistants in their Lakota language. "Kelan, you will take us out to the east side of the house," Dan directed.

Ty walked with the men through the kitchen and out the door. They crossed the porch and went over to the grass. Kelan had warned him ahead of time to leave his weapons in the safe in his room. "Please, remove your shirts and your shoes," Dan requested. "You must stand barefoot upon the ground."

One of his assistants set out four clay dishes with shallow bowls of sand on the ground nearby. Next to that, he set out a few dozen clumps of bound and dried herbs. The other assistant brought over two drums that were made from wood and animal skins, each of a size that a single person could carry and play it.

The first assistant handed Dan a fifth clay bowl of sand and one of the herb sticks. He lit the herbs then blew out the flame, letting the stick smoke. Dan took a large owl feather from his pouch and pushed smoke in the four directions, north, west, south, and east, chanting in Lakota.

"We will begin now by purifying ourselves and our tools so that we can be protected from the things that we wish to clear from this house and its grounds. There is nothing you must do other than fill your mind with thoughts that give you joy and for which you are grateful."

He went over to his assistants, who remained fully dressed and still wore their moccasins. Moving from the ground, up the left leg over the center of the first assistant's body, to his head, he used the feather to puff the smoke to his left. As he descended from the head down the torso to the right, the shaman pushed the smoke off to the right side. As he stirred the smoke, he chanted in a singsong voice words that Ty didn't understand but which he found wonderfully comforting.

"Why do they get to keep their shoes and shirts on?" he asked Kelan ash the shaman repeated the smoke gestures over the assistant's back.

"They are wearing leather and cotton, materials from plants and animals of the earth. Plus, they've likely been purified before coming onto the property. This is a reminder to the spirits to protect and care for them as they help to heal this space and its occupants. We are in need of a much deeper cleansing. It is good to be connected to Mother Earth as the bad energies release their hold on us."

"Why smoke?" Ty asked, whispering so he wouldn't break Dan's concentration.

"Smoke moves between dimensions. It transports our thoughts to the spirit realm. It's a link between the here and the hereafter."

Dan repeated his ministrations on the second assistant, then stood while the first assistant performed that service for him. And then it was Ty and Kelan's turn. The smoke smelled of sage and left him a little light headed. When the humans had been treated, Dan purified the tools he would use for the ceremony.

"You may dress again."

Once they'd put their shirts and boots back on, he and Kelan carried two clay bowls and followed Dan back down to the basement.

"Dan, this isn't the lowest part of the house. Do you want to start in the lower basement?" Ty asked.

"No. We will begin here, then move upstairs. When we are finished, we will do the bunker and move outside through the tunnel to the grounds. If you feel overwhelmed by what happens here, you may sit down or go back outside." He and the assistants opened all of the windows in the basement. "The spirits have lost their way in here. We will orient them again and send them home to the Creator."

The assistants lit the herb logs in each of the clay dishes, then set them in the four compass directions as far apart as possible. They took up the small drums and waited for the shaman to begin his chant as he moved the smoke strategically about the room.

* * *

Later that afternoon, Ivy had been banished to the den—with the girls and Val—to wait for her parents. If the afternoon had gone on much longer, she feared Val would have broken out a round of charades just to keep the mood calm. It felt silly hiding in there, but Kathy and Dennis had convinced her to let them be the ones to admit her parents and show them to their room. They felt it would set the proper tone for them to be met by people who worked for the team and who respected Kit.

The doorbell rang. "Shh-shh. The ogres are here," Val said.

"They're not ogres," Ivy corrected him with a small laugh. She started for the door but Val stepped in front of it with his arms spread wide.

"You can't go out there yet. Let's see if Dennis and Kathy survive their encounter first."

"Val—"

"He's right," Mandy told her, drawing her back into the room. "Sure it's pomp and circumstance, but it sends the message that you and Kit and Casey are important to us. Kathy is going to tell them to come downstairs when they're settled. You can't go to them, Ivy. They have to come to you. It's a power thing."

"I agree. It's a non-verbal cue that sets dominance," Eden added. "Works the same way with dogs."

Ivy looked at Casey, who was big-eyed and pale. She crossed the room to give her a hug. "I just want to get this over with. Did you tell Kit they're here?" she asked Val.

"Yep. He's on his way up."

There was a sound in the large storage closet, then the door opened and Kit came out. He looked at Ivy and Casey, then grinned. "Showtime!"

Ivy caught her breath. He looked relaxed, carefree even, as if two ogres hadn't just entered his house. This was what he did for a living, she realized—face down the evil elements of life. He came over to her and held her face.

"Iv, there's no point cataloging what happened in the past. Now is the time to look at them with adult eyes and adult hearts and see what their hearts say back. The rest is done. It's over. It hurt them. It hurt us. It hurt Casey. But look how strong you are. Both of you. And the future, for a fact, will be one we're all comfortable with, no matter what that means."

Ivy nodded. She pulled Casey close so Kit could hug them both. "Ready?" she asked them.

"Affirmative." Kit smiled.

Ivy felt full of dread as they walked down the

hallway, despite his cheerleading. Kit was walking between her and Casey, holding their hands. Her daughter leaned forward and looked over at her. "Mom, can we take them over to the diner tomorrow?"

"I think that would be nice. Maybe they'd like to see what we've done."

Mandy had set out some games in the living room in preparation for what might be a long, tense wait for Ivy's parents to come down from their room. Casey, Fee, and Eden got involved in a game of Apples to Apples. Ivy couldn't sit still. She paced back and forth from the hall to the patio doors until Kit came up behind her and wrapped his arms around her.

"I got you. Lean on me."

She drew a deep breath, then tried to relax back against him, her hand gripping his wrist. A commotion on the bridge upstairs caught their attention. She and Kit turned to see her parents midway on the steps, at the landing that overlooked the living room. Her mom gasped when she saw them, pausing to hold the banister in a white-knuckled grip. Her dad stood next to her. Looking over the room, he nodded at her and Kit.

CHAPTER NINE

A strange flood of emotion overtook Ivy. Joy, fear, guilt, sorrow. And hope. She looked up at Kit, who met her glance with his own troubled gaze. He took her hand and led her to the foyer. She didn't know what to do. Greet them like any other unknown visitor? Hug them? Shake hands with them?

Her mom, it seemed, was having the same quandary. She stood before Ivy with a hand over her mouth, her eyes filling with tears. "Mom..." Ivy choked out before opening her arms to hug her. Ivy felt as if she'd jumped back in time to her younger self. She was zinged with sharp flashes of all the memories that floated like razorblades in her heart. The fear, the hurt, the humiliation. *Put it away*, Kit had said. How? How was she to do that when it was still so raw?

Her mom pulled free and leaned back to look at

her. "Oh, Ivy. You are such a beautiful sight for my eyes."

"You too, Mom."

Her mom turned to Kit, who just finished shaking hands with her father. She took hold of his hand in both of hers. "Thank you. Thank you for being brave enough to invite us. I know we have a great deal to discuss. It's a short weekend, and a hectic one, too, but I hope we'll have a chance to talk a bit."

Kit smiled at her, then pulled her into his arms. "We'll make time."

Ivy looked around them at her father. "Dad."

"Mom's right. You sure are beautiful."

"Thank you. I'm glad you came."

"Kit made it easy for us."

"Was the trip difficult?" she asked them, grateful for a neutral subject.

"Not at all, dear," her mom answered. She leaned close to Ivy and whispered, "He flew us out on a private jet. And the SUV that drove us up here was comfy, although the men who drove it were not very talkative." She looked back at Kit. "It was thoughtful of you. But you needn't have gone to such trouble. We would have come on our own."

"I know you would have." He smiled at her. "You know why I know?" She shook her head. "Because it was time for this."

"It's past time. Where's my granddaughter?"

"Casey," Kit called. She got up from her seat on the floor by the coffee table.

"Grandma, Grandpa," she greeted them tentatively.

"Look at her, Adam. She's all grown up. And so pretty." At twelve, Casey was nearly as tall as her grandmother. She gave her elders a cautious smile. Ivy wrapped an arm around her. Helen looked between Ivy and Kit, then back at Casey. "She's a perfect mix of both of you. Her mom's features and her dad's coloring."

"Are you hungry?" Ivy asked her parents.

"Starving. Your father wouldn't eat the airport food. And you know he doesn't like fast food, so we didn't stop on the way up here. I packed us a lunch, but we ate that on the plane."

Ivy led them into the living room. "Well, good. We have a big dinner planned in honor of your visit."

"This is a nice house. It's been expanded since we lived in town. Didn't it used to belong to the Bladens?" Adam asked.

"It still belongs to Ty."

"Huh. So you live here, off his dime?"

Kit stopped. Took a breath. Then faced his soon-to-be father-in-law. "You're outta line, Adam," he said quietly. Ivy had never heard him use that tone of voice. "I suggest you don't start handing out insults five minutes into your visit." He stepped into Adam's space. "You're here to spend an important weekend with Ivy and Casey, but I can take you out that door just as easily as I brought you in it."

"You haven't changed. You're still the hoodlum

you always were." He looked at Ivy then back at Kit. "Did you give her any choice about her future? Or did you just demand it would go the way you wanted?"

"Like you ever gave her any choices—least any that didn't mean killing my daughter?"

Ivy's father squared off with him. "It's because of you Ivy had to hide. You stole her from us."

"Oh, God. Adam, please. Please. We agreed—" Ivy's mom tried to calm their escalating tempers. Ivy didn't spare her a glance; she couldn't take her eyes off her father and Kit. They were face to face now. Kit had grown since she'd last seen the two of them together. Her dad, at six feet, towered over her and her mom, using his size to intimidate them. It had always worked before, but now Kit was half a head taller and a good bit wider. She feared Kit was going to eviscerate him.

"I'm why. *I'm why*," Kit repeated, his voice a hoarse whisper. "You wouldn't let me near her. You wouldn't let my phone calls get through to her. You kept my letters from her. I had to go AWOL to see her, but you'd put a restraining order on me. You took them from me and left them to fend for themselves. My *woman*. My *daughter*. They could have died because of you." He looked over at Ivy.

Ivy couldn't breathe, couldn't move. Even her tears were like crystals at the edges of her eyes.

Kit stepped away, then faced Adam again. "You never tried to find her. You just left them out there in the world, as I did, because of you. But you know what? They didn't need either of us. Did you know that Ivy has a degree in business administration? Did you know she runs a very successful small business in town? Did you know Casey is a fucking math whiz? Did you know she's a brown belt in karate?" He bowed his head and sucked in air. "No. You didn't know. Because you didn't care to know."

"Boy, you always could pile on the bullshit," her father countered. "How the hell was I supposed to know where she went? How was I supposed to find her when she didn't want to be found?" He pointed in Ivy's direction. "She knew where we were. She knew our address. Our phone number. She never once tried to reach out to us."

"You really expected her to do that? When every convo you'd had with her since learning of her pregnancy was about how to get rid of Casey?" Kit shook his head. He paced a few steps to his side, standing between her and her dad. "You were an adult. The burden was on your shoulders. You should have tried and tried and tried. Then tried again. They're your flesh and blood. They're my world. I would give my life for them." He looked Adam in the eyes. "Would you?"

Adam shut his eyes. When he opened them, Ivy saw a terrible sorrow. He had the look of a man who'd wished for death, but kept living, day after day. Worn and beaten. "I did. I've paid for my sins every minute, every hour, every day and week and month and year that's passed since this started." His shoulders slumped. "I just want it to end."

Ivy choked on a sob. She slipped past Kit and wrapped her arms around her father. Together, they cried. Ivy's tears came from a bottomless well, one she'd dragged around with her for years, into which her every hope and dream had fallen into and drowned.

After a few minutes, her dad straightened. He gripped Ivy's shoulders, gave her a squeeze. He nodded at her, then at Kit. "We'll get our things and leave."

"I'm not leaving, Adam," Ivy's mom said, rejecting his edict.

"No one's going," Ivy whispered through her tears.

"She's right," Kit said. "We start again. We start now. What happened happened. We can pick a different future. We can make that future together."

Ivy sniffled. Her father reached into his pocket and handed her his clean hankie. She laughed when she saw it. How many times had he done that when she was a kid?

She turned to her mom, and the tears started again. "Mom, we have so much to catch up on."

"We do. Yes, we do. But first, I have to say that your father can't stand alone in the blame. I didn't speak up. I didn't fight for you the way I should have. We worried about such superficial things—we cared more about them than about you." She shook her head. "And all those people we feared would judge us or obstruct your father's career, they're just gone anyway. Our counselor has helped us see how we let fear drive our lives. Your invitation couldn't have come at a better time. I'm grateful you thought of us. After everything." She hugged Ivy, then reached for Kit's hand. "Thank you."

"You're welcome, Mrs. Banks."

"Kit"—she straightened and faced him—"you're marrying our daughter in two days. I think it's time you called me Mom and Adam Dad, if you're willing. Otherwise, Helen and Adam."

Kit held out his hand to Adam. Ivy loved that half-grin he had on his face. "You ever imagine I'd be calling you 'Dad'?"

"No. I've spent the last thirteen years imagining killing you." Adam shook his hand. "But now I'm thinking it might be nice to have a son. I've never had one before. I'll probably be bad at it."

"I guess we're even, then. I never had a dad."

Adam laughed and clapped him on the back. "So, daughter, are you going to feed us tonight?"

Ivy swiped her hands across her face. She looked around, realizing how silent the room had become once her dad and Kit started in on each other. They were alone. She was glad Casey had been spared the worst of that scene.

"Yes. Let me just clean up a bit. Mom—there are two bathrooms in the hall on either side of the living room if you want to freshen up."

"I'll go see where everyone is," Kit said. "We'll meet back here in a few minutes. Dad"—Kit paused and grinned—"there's a stocked bar. Help yourself." He took Ivy's hand and led her out of the living room. Inside their room, he pulled her into his arms. She drew a deep breath and rested her head against his chest.

"You worked a miracle today, Kit. I don't know how you did it, but you put the pieces back together."

"We'll see. I think it's a good start."

"Far better than I could have dreamed. I hate to say it, but you were right about this. I didn't realize what a weight it was for me, for us."

He smiled down at her and tucked a strand of hair behind her ear. "I've told you you're my life, haven't I?"

"I'm so lucky to have you." Ivy had to blink more tears away. "I don't know what's wrong with me. I can't seem to stop crying."

"You look beautiful to me. You can cry the whole weekend away if you want, as long as you still marry me."

Ivy gave him a wet laugh as she kissed his lips. "Go find everyone. Tell them it's safe. Check on Casey, too, 'kay? I'll be out in a few minutes."

"Roger that."

CHAPTER TEN

Kit had noticed the guys crowded in the kitchen as he'd walked Ivy to their room. When he stepped into the room, conversations stopped and all eyes turned to him. He held his hands out. "Really? Are you hiding in here?"

"Fuck yeah," Blade told him. "Eden said some shit was goin' down. I don't see blood. Everything cool?"

"Yeah. Where's Case?"

"I'm here, Dad." She leaned around Angel on the bench at the table.

"Come here," Kit called her over.

Angel lifted her over him and set her on her feet. She rushed to hug Kit. He patted her back. "Sorry about that. I didn't mean for it all to go down like that, but I'm glad it did, glad we got it over with." He looked at his daughter. "We've decided to move forward as a family. I'd like you to try to get to know your grandparents while they're here. Let's make good use of this weekend."

She set her jaw and glared up at him through sparkling eyes. "They made Mom cry again."

He put his hand on her head. "They didn't. The situation did. It's a lot of emotion to work through. I'd rather Mom cry than suck it up and tough it out. With this at least." He sent a glance around the room. "Thanks for giving us space."

"You know, Kit, I don't think you would have found common ground as quickly or as easily had Dan and his crew not cleared the house today," Blade told him.

Kit smiled, remembering how noisy the space clearing had been that morning with the drums and the chanting. It had chased Owen out of his room. He'd stumbled into the kitchen, barefoot and wearing only jeans, to fill a mug with Kathy's dark coffee like an addict jonessing for a fix. He'd taken a long draw of the hot liquid, then grumbled, *Jesus Mother of God, tell me you hear that, too.*" He'd glared at Kit over his mug. *"I can't be that hungover."*

Kit looked at Blade. "Does the house feel different to you?"

He nodded. "It's not hard to breathe in the basement anymore. In fact, I'm thinking about putting in some offices down there."

Shocked, Kit looked over at Kelan, who was standing with the shaman and his two assistants. He went over to hold his hand out. "I don't know what you did, or how you did it, Dan, but I appreciate the help here."

The shaman looked at Kit with a penetrating gaze as he took his hand. Kit felt uncomfortably exposed. "There is more healing to be done, but the shadows were happy to go. Tonight, after we eat, we'll smoke a pipe. I'll say a prayer over the warriors, then the men. Tomorrow, I'll say a prayer for the women. I'll cleanse the five of you, then on Saturday, I'll prepare the room for the ceremony. It will be a good way to begin your new lives."

"I didn't realize it would take so much of your time," Kit said.

When the shaman didn't answer, Kelan did. "Adjusting the energy of a place takes the time it takes. It's important that it be handled thoroughly."

Kit put a hand on Kelan's shoulder. "Thanks, K." He looked around, but didn't see Owen among those hiding in the kitchen. "Where's Owen?"

"He's keeping Adam company."

"Oh, hell."

* * *

Owen poured shallow amber streams of Balcones into two glasses. As requested, he put ice in Adam's. He pushed the iced glass toward their visitor, then tipped his glass to Adam before taking a sip.

"So, you're a friend of Kit's and Ty's?" Adam asked.

"Nope. I'm their boss."

"And what is it that your company does?"

"We run an international security services consultancy. We've made Ty Holt's house our western headquarters."

Adam tilted his head back and gave him a mistrustful look. "Ty's last name is Bladen."

"It was." He didn't elaborate.

"So, tell me about Kit. What's your opinion of him?"

Owen fixed his gaze on Adam's eyes. "There are many ways to take the measure of a man. Kit meets every one of them. And he's a helluva team lead."

"When did he start working for you?"

"When he left the Army this summer."

"So you haven't known him very long, then."

Owen got off the stool where he sat next to Adam at the bar. "You'll soon meet the rest of our team. And when you do, you'll know a whole lot more about your soon-to-be son-in-law. Takes a true man to be a leader they'd follow. If I'm ever lucky enough to have a daughter, a man like Kit's the only one I'd let marry her." He smiled at Adam. Seeing the tension settle over the man's face, he guessed it wasn't one of his warmest gestures. "Enjoy your weekend, Mr. Banks." Owen went over to one of the armchairs in the far corner and took a seat. It was the best seat in the house to watch what would come next.

* * *

Kit came into the room from the hallway. He looked from Owen to Adam. They weren't sitting together. Whether that was a good thing remained unclear. Adam held up his glass. "Owen shared his Balcones stash."

Kit helped himself to Owen's bottle, which still sat on the bar. Helen rejoined them. Adam stood up. She smiled at Kit, then hugged him. He looked down at the tiny woman clinging to him, entirely uncertain what to do. He finally decided to behave as if women hugged him all the time. He put his hands on her back and patted her.

"Thank you." She looked up at him. "You were so brave to make this happen." She went over and put her arm around Adam. "We would have regretted missing Ivy's marriage for the rest of our lives."

"You're welcome. Mom." He grinned.

The other guys spilled into the room, causing a dizzying few minutes of introductions as they met the team, their girls, Mr. Broken Knife, and his assistants. The only person missing was Max. Kit hadn't heard if he was going to be able to get in. They probably wouldn't know until he showed or didn't.

Ivy came in last. She had an arm around Casey and a smile in her eyes as she searched for and found him. He smiled back at her. The two of them came straight over. Casey went to stand with Helen and Adam. Ivy put her arms around his neck then kissed him. "I love you." She hugged both of her parents, then held

Casey's hand as they started a conversation.

Val served the women drinks. Iced tea for Helen and Casey, Shiraz for Ivy. Kit looked at the sniper, feeling a little shell-shocked at the changes that had happened today. Val smiled at him and did a fist-bump.

CHAPTER ELEVEN

Selena stepped out of the elevator into the weapons room the morning of the wedding. The bunker was empty; the guys were upstairs preparing for the big event. The muscles Owen had brought in as escort for Kit's in-laws were at their posts, giving the team some breathing room for the festivities.

Selena opened the door into the operations room as a big guy stepped through from the opposite door. His facial piercings, dark, shaggy hair, and several days' growth of beard were a stark contrast to his black and white penguin suit and black bow tie. Max Cameron.

For a minute, neither spoke. They just squared off. He broke the silence. "Selena. You look different than I expected."

She pushed her hair behind her shoulder. Why the hell had she let Casey and Fiona talk her into wearing it loose? "Huh. It's the flower."

A little smile softened Max's features. "Yeah, that's it. I'm Max, by the way." They shook hands.

"Kit know you're here?" she asked.

"Yep."

"I'm glad you made it."

He sent her a curious glance. "Why?"

She shrugged. "The guys felt it wouldn't be a party without you."

He made a face. "That's me. A metric fuck ton of fun. Where's Greer?"

"Dunno. I just came to check on things before it all goes to hell." Truthfully, she was hiding. Gigs like this weren't her cuppa. "Well, guess I'll head up." Into the fray.

"Sel…" He stopped her. She looked back at him from the doorway to the weapons room. "You sitting at my table?"

"I doubt it. I'm at the kids' table." She'd specifically requested that assignment from Ivy.

"We'll see about that. I don't think Owen put you in silks to have you wipe infant noses."

"He didn't put me in silks."

"Didn't he? What the fuck are you wearing?"

"I paid for this."

"Sure you did. Owen's good at mind freaks—or hadn't you figured that out?"

The elevator opened behind her. Blade and Kit came into the room, laughing until they saw her. Blade whistled. "You clean up pretty good, Selena."

"Thanks, Blade."

Kit put his arm around her shoulder. "Glad to see you decided to join us. Ivy was worried about you."

"I'll be there."

Some of the other guys came in from the conference room hall. The small ops room was too tight for all of them. Selena pulled back and stood against the wall, watching the guys greet Max.

"So who's next to bite to dust?" Max asked, looking around the room. "You, Rocco?"

Rocco was leaning against the opposite wall. His arms were folded. He looked at Max but didn't answer him.

"No. That'd be me and Eden," Blade said. He sent Rocco a glance. "Not that it's a race or anything."

Rocco shrugged. "We're cool." Selena had seen him becoming increasingly withdrawn over the last two weeks. She couldn't blame him. Weddings weren't her thing either.

"I'm going up to check on the girls," she said.

"We'll be behind you shortly," Kit told her. "I have something I want to give Ivy."

Upstairs, Kathy's helpers were making last-minute adjustments to the tables outside. Eden was casually walking Tank around, having him check out the space yet again. There was a huge awning set up outside with several tables that each sat six. For a smallish wedding, there were more people attending than Selena had expected.

On the far side of the tent, rows of white folding

chairs were set up in front of a flower-covered archway and podium. Greer's sound system was placed in a strategic corner. Japanese lanterns had been strung overhead to brighten the long patio for dancers once night fell. Everywhere Selena looked, there were flowers and bows and feminine touches. It looked as if a herd of fairies had sneezed magic dust across the space. For only having a few weeks to put this shindig together, Ivy had done a hell of a job.

She went farther down the hall on her way to Ivy's room. The kitchen was buzzing with workers. Kit had gotten Ivy to relent and bring in her caterers for tonight, using her menu. They'd brought with them several wait staff. Greer had cleared them and Eden had had Tank do his thing on their vehicles and everything they brought into the house. Still, there were so many moving parts that Selena couldn't fully relax.

Casey came out of her room wearing the sundress Val had picked out for her and her new boots. She had a little lip-gloss on and it looked like maybe a dash of blush on her cheeks. And mascara.

"How do I look?" she asked Selena, doing a quick circle.

"Stunning. You ready for this?"

Casey grinned. "I'm so ready."

"How's your mom doing?"

She made a little face. "I thought it was safer to be out here."

Mandy came out of Casey's room with a curling

iron and hurried into Ivy's, waving at Selena as she went past. Selena squeezed Casey's shoulder. "Good call. I'm going to check on her. If it's safe, I'll call you in."

Ivy's room looked like a clothes bomb had detonated. Fiona and Mandy were standing next to Ivy at the vanity in the bathroom. Fiona was making some final retouches on Ivy's complicated braiding, fitting tiny sprigs of flowers into what looked a basket weave of Ivy's dark hair that circled the crown of her hair. Everywhere the strands crossed other strands, there were flowers or pearls. On her dark hair, the effect was beautiful. Below the horizontal rows of braiding, her hair hung loose.

Ivy was grilling Mandy on a list of activities. "The tables are set up," Mandy said. "All the place cards have been set. The bar is set up. Greer's ready with the music. It's all done. All of it. I had the same list you have, Ivy. All that's left is for you to walk out there and get married."

"Is the justice of the peace here?" Ivy asked.

"Not yet. But he will be soon," Selena told her.

"Selena! Look at you!" Ivy got up and hurried over to her. She took Selena's hands and made her walk forward. "I love this outfit. I'm so glad you picked this one."

"Yeah. I've had three guys ask me to sit with them."

"Um. No." Ivy shook her head. "Try five of them."

"That's ridiculous. I'm glad you're putting me at the kids' table."

Ivy winced. "I didn't, actually."

"What?"

"There is no kids' table. There's just Zavi and Casey. Casey will be with us. And Zavi will be with Mandy and Rocco."

Selena crossed her arms and frowned down at the bride. "Who did you put me with?"

"Owen."

"Seriously? Owen?"

"And Val."

"Crap."

"And a couple of my friends. You met them at the party." Ivy looked at her. "And Max."

Selena forced herself to smile.

Ivy's eyes narrowed. "What are you doing?" she asked.

"That's my happy smile. This is your day. I'll sit wherever the hell you want me."

Ivy's phone rang. She hurried into the other room to answer it. "Hi, Kit. No, you can't see me. Okay. Just a minute." She came back into the room and pulled her robe on. "I'll be right back."

"Is everything all right?"

Ivy nodded. "Kit just asked if I could come out and see him for a minute."

Ivy hurried out into the hallway, shutting the door behind her. The women gathered in the short hall that led to the bedroom door, hoping to overhear their conversation. Ivy's mom waited a little distance from them.

"What's going on?" Mandy asked, looking at Fiona, who was closest to the door.

Fiona shrugged. "I can't hear."

"I know what it is," Helen's voice came softly into the group. "When Kit invited us out for the wedding, I told him I was going to bring Ivy my grandmother's diamond and aquamarine earrings. Something blue, you know. He said he was going to have a necklace made to match." Ivy's mom had a soft, wistful smile and eyes that were impossibly sad. "I can't believe I couldn't see in the boy who stole my daughter's heart, the man he could become. What a fool I was."

Mandy gave Helen a hug. "It's not like life comes with a user guide. You're here now. Kit's right—don't look back."

The door opened. Ivy and Casey stepped in. Ivy was wearing a beautiful pearl necklace with a big, tear-shaped, light blue stone hanging from the center. The necklace would hang perfectly in the V of her wedding dress. Casey also wore a new pearl necklace. Hers was shorter, made from smaller pearls. Instead of a teardrop pendant, her center blue stone was a round, bezel-set stone. It was a beautiful complement to her pale coloring.

Ivy's mom came forward and hugged her daughter. "Look, Mom, it matches the earrings you gave me." She glanced down at her necklace. "Kit said he picked the teardrop because it would symbolize the transformation of our tears from something sad to something beautiful."

Selena was more moved than she wanted to admit. "Wow. It's gonna be weird when he's handing my ass to me somewhere down the line to remember the bastard has such a poetic side." The girls laughed.

Ivy hugged Casey. "And look what he gave Casey. Isn't it beautiful?" She touched her daughter's necklace.

"I've never had something this nice," Casey said, reverently holding the necklace forward for the others to inspect it. Ivy wiped at her tears.

"Okay. Enough of that." Mandy grabbed her hand and led her back into the bathroom. "You're going to ruin your makeup!"

"Casey, come help me straighten the room," Helen called her granddaughter over.

Selena slipped out of the room. The estrogen was playing havoc with her nerves. She thought she'd head down and see if Eden needed any help. She saw Eden, Tank, and Blade step out the front door as she came into the main hallway. At the far end of the hall, Owen was just stepping out of his wing. He wore the same black and white tux Max had. His blond hair was brushed back from his face. His jaw was clean-shaven. His eyes caught hers.

Selena cursed silently. Facing him was like staring down a wolf in a long chute where you couldn't escape or look away.

When they were separated by the space of the

living room, his cold blue eyes, as pale as Ivy's new aquamarine, made a slow pass over her outfit, snagging on the bare skin her jacket revealed before returning to her eyes. She thought about dodging him by stepping into the living room or walking out the front door, but that felt cowardly. They walked straight to each other like a clamp slowly being tightened. Selena's heels made her almost six feet tall, but even in them she still had to look up to see his eyes.

"Nice outfit."

"Val chose it."

"Of course."

"I hate the freaking rose."

He smiled, and what that did to his face made her stop breathing. In an effort to return things to normalcy, she drew up the hems of her pants and showed him her ankle holsters and calf KA-BAR sheath. And…judging from his reaction, that was a stupid thing to do. Great. Like a real woman would ever do something so graceless. Or an operative something so needless. He made her feel thirteen again.

"Do you ever really let your hair down?" he asked, his voice rough around the edges.

"Not when I'm on a 24-7 assignment, like this."

"And that, Selena, is why you're here."

He stepped away from her, moving into the living room. She went in the opposite direction, making straight for the front door. Only half an hour now before the ceremony. She'd make a quick circuit of the area, then come back to follow behind Ivy as she walked outside.

* * *

Ivy opened her bedroom door a few minutes later. Her father stood there. "It's time," he said. He took her hand and led her out into the sitting room. "For some reason, I feel as nervous as the day I married your mom." He looked at his wife. "Maybe it's because that was the best day of my life."

"Dad—"

"I can't believe you're letting me give you away, letting me be part of this day."

"Dad…" Ivy couldn't find words that didn't involve choking on a mouthful of tears.

"Don't get her started, Adam," her mom said as she came out of the room. "We've only just gotten her calmed down. You're beautiful, sweetheart." She kissed Ivy's cheek, then hugged Casey. "I'm going to go sit down."

"We'll go with you, Helen," Mandy said as she made a last adjustment to Ivy's hair.

Fiona hugged Ivy, then handed her the bouquet. "I can't wait to watch Kit's face when he sees you."

"Ready, Casey?" Ivy asked.

"Mom, I've been ready for this since I found dad's first letter to you in your jewelry box."

Ivy laughed and hugged her daughter. "You know

the best part of today? Besides having your grandparents with us? With the wedding happening now, and not before you were born, you get to be here too to see us get married."

"I like that."

"Ready?" her dad asked. She nodded. He tucked a hankie in his hand. "Just in case either of us needs it." She smiled and looped her arm through his. They moved down the hallway and into the living room. When Greer saw them, he winked at Casey, then started the wedding song. Casey stepped out first, moving slowly down the aisle toward her father.

Ivy, still in the shadows of the living room, could see Kit outside in the sunshine. He looked as beautiful to her now as he had the day he'd graduated. She looked up at her dad, thinking how different his loving hold on her now was from his angry grasp then. As if reading her thoughts, he nodded.

They started forward. Ivy could barely hear the music for the way her heart hammered in her ears. Casey was standing in front of Mandy. Kit was standing next to Ty. His team and all the people she'd become so fond of came to their feet. Fee was next to her mom. Ivy started smiling, and try as she might, she couldn't stop. She looked at Kit. He wasn't smiling. Far from it. The muscles bunched in the corners of his cheeks. He watched her as if she were the very breath he breathed.

When her father handed her off to him, Ivy smiled at Kit, warmed by the heat in his eyes. How different this was, their being joined not torn apart. He leaned forward and kissed her cheek, then whispered, "I love you, Ivy mine."

ABOUT THE AUTHOR

Elaine Levine lives on the plains of Colorado with her husband, a middle-aged parrot, and a rescued pit bull/bullmastiff mix. In addition to writing the Red Team contemporary romantic suspense series, she is the author of several books in the historical western series, Men of Defiance. Visit her online at ElaineLevine.com for more information about her upcoming books. She loves hearing from readers! Contact her at elevine@elainelevine.com.

CPSIA information can be obtained at www.ICGtesting.com
Printed in the USA
LVOW11s1337080614

389113LV00001B/27/P